Latimer's Justice

Dean Latimer has a reputation for staying cool under fire and being handy with both his fists and guns. So, when the US marshal needs him to help a lady prove her brother innocent of a murder charge he is the perfect man for the job.

Baxterville though is run by three crooked men with gunslingers backing their play and when Latimer tries to save the innocent man he ends up accused of murder and running for his life.

But Dean Latimer didn't earn his good name by being meek. When it comes to a fight, there's hell to pay and no refunds for the losers.

Latimer's Justice

Terrell L. Bowers

A Black Horse Western

ROBERT HALE · LONDON

© Terrell L. Bowers 2013
First published in Great Britain 2013

ISBN 978-0-7198-0996-5

Robert Hale Limited
Clerkenwell House
Clerkenwell Green
London EC1R 0HT

www.halebooks.com

Typeset by
Derek Doyle & Associates, Shaw Heath
Printed and bound in Great Britain by
CPI Antony Rowe, Chippenham and Eastbourne

CHAPTER ONE

There was a lot of money to be made in the 1850s with a steamboat, making the run from St Louis to Miami, 270 miles all along the Missouri River – often referred to as The Big Muddy. The burgeoning passenger and shipping traffic spawned dozens of companies all competing for the immense amount of wealth that was there for the taking.

Captain Francis T. Belt purchased the *Saluda*, a side-wheeler steamboat for a song, but the singing was not as loud and melodious as he had hoped. With little effort, he gathered a full load of more than 200 passengers, many of them Mormons from Wales and England, on their way to Council Bluffs, where they would take the long trip across country to the Salt Lake Valley and their Zion.

However, the spring of 1852 had been wet and cold, causing the river to run at flood levels. It was a swift and powerful force of Nature to be reckoned with, especially along the promontory above Lexington, Missouri. To maneuver in to the main waterway the boats had to traverse a bend in the channel, a difficult strait which was currently littered with clumps of ice and running a full head of muddy water.

On 7 April, Captain Belt pitted his steamboat against the raging flow. The *Saluda* was a double-engine, double-boiler, but she did not have the power to match the awesome torrent of water and swirling blocks of ice. Time and again Belt urged his steamboat ahead and attempted to battle up and around the bend. Each effort was a dismal failure, as the old steamboat simply didn't have the power to buck the powerful current. After two days of futility, along with suffering ridicule from a crowd of people from town who had gathered to watch each failed effort from the shore, Captain Belt declared it was time to do or die. He ordered the safety valves be locked down and the fireboxes filled to capacity.

He called for every bit of steam the old lady could produce and vowed they were going to make it around the damnable point or else!

The *Saluda* built up a full head of steam and started off, paddles turning with maximum thrust, the engine practically screaming ... and then the boilers exploded and blew the ship apart!

Dean Latimer was standing next to his older sister and brother, along with his father and mother, all of them clinging to the side railing, hopeful they would finally advance beyond the near impassable bend.

The sudden and terrifying concussion shattered Dean's world. Everything went black before his eyes and Dean felt himself launched high into the air. He returned to earth to land on a cold, hard bed which jarred every bone in his body. It seemed that hours passed before he managed to suck in enough air to fill his lungs and get his heart beating again. He forced his eyes open and blinked against the glaring sun. Beyond the thunderous ringing in his ears he could make out cries of pain, shock and despair.

'Dad?' He squeaked out the word, eventually able to get his voice to work.

'Easy there, little pardnuh,' a gruff yet strangely compassionate voice said. Moving to block the sun, a man leaned over Dean's body. He had a shaggy beard and black hair stuck out from under a woolen hat. A man of average build and height, he grinned through several missing teeth. 'You're gonna' be jus' fine, sonny boy.'

Dean managed to rise up on to his elbows, stunned to discover he was well beyond the bank of the river. He looked about and gasped in horror.

The realization of what had happened caused Dean to grow sick. He turned over and vomited, while his mind stuggled to cope with the gruesome scene. There were bodies lying about – some were only large pieces – with smoldering wood and metal scattered about. The river had already swallowed up most of the steamboat, leaving nothing but a few slabs of the hull and a mass of twisted metal still visible in the water. The cries of woe and sorrow were everywhere, coming from those on shore and a few still in the water.

'You don't need to be a-seeing this,' the scruffy-looking man at his side told him. 'I'll get you someplace dry and warm, till we learn what happened to the rest of your family.'

Dean could not think and pinched his eyes closed, trying desperately to blot out the horrific scene from his sight. The image embedded before his mind's eye was of the red streams that had formed along the bank – the blood from the many who had just died, including a few of the spectators who had come to see Captain Belt try his luck against the mighty river. The powerful explosion had sent parts of the ship flying into the crowd like shrapnel, injuring and even killing some of them.

'Dad and Mom?' Dean sobbed. 'My sister and brother?'

'I'll be a checking on that for you, pardnuh,' his rescuer promised. 'Let's just find a place for you to warm up.'

Dean risked taking a final look at the tragedy. He needed no one to tell him he was alone in the world.

It was an odd quirk of fate that he had been standing atop a riveted iron plate, used to support one of the ropes to secure the ship while in dock. He had been propelled to shore like being shot from a catapult. The only reason he had no broken bones was because he had landed in someone's shrubbery. The thick bushes had worked like a pile of mattresses to break his fall.

'Name's Rambling George Brody, but everyone calls me Ramble,' the man carrying him explained. 'Don't you be fretting, sonny. Soon as we get you in a warm bed, I'll mosey back and find out what I can about your kin. What's your name?'

'Latimer,' Dean told him. 'There were five of us.'

'Got it. Latimer,' Ramble repeated. 'I'll sure 'nuff find out if any of your kin made it to shore.'

Dean was ten, old enough to know it was unmanly to cry, but the tears burned his eyes and a couple drops of moisture escaped to slide down his cheeks. A new life in a new world, his parents had promised. They would have started up a farm or an orchard and been a part of a new community, a piece of the American Dream.

Except the dream has become a nightmare, Dean decided woefully. There was little hope that any of his family had survived. He was alone, completely alone in an unfamiliar land, without a friend or relative in the world.

*

Rambling George Brody was a combination of gad-about and drifter. He did everything from shag freight to break horses and even worked in a saloon on occasion. With Dean Latimer being an orphan, Ramble took charge of his care. The boy already knew how to read and write, so his education grew to include chores of all kinds and tending to their campsite and animals. When Ramble killed game, Latimer was instructed on how to skin the animal and clean and tan the hide. When Ramble tended bar, Latimer would run drinks to tables and help clean up after the last patron was gone.

Ramble especially wanted Latimer to be able to handle himself. By the time he was twelve Latimer could shoot better than most men. Ramble also had a habit of promoting wrestling or boxing contests, pitting Latimer against bigger boys so he could get someone to wager against him. With the tricks Ramble taught Dean, plus what he learned on his own, he was soon pinning or knocking down youths who were considerably bigger and stronger than himself. As for the shooting competition, Ramble often bet someone a meal or a couple dollars that Latimer was a better shot than whoever they could find to pit against him.

Eventually Ramble landed a permanent job for them at a way station. Dean got to know the stage drivers and most of them became aware of the boy's talent with his fists or a gun. They often teamed with

Ramble to make wagers against some arrogant jack or braggart who thought he could best a skinny teenage boy. Most often, Dean's opponent discovered it was best not to judge the measure of a man by his size or youthful appearance.

The war between the Confederacy and Union came, yet had little effect on their position, as the express companies continued to haul supplies and passengers. Dean Latimer grew to be a man and continued to work with Ramble, tending horses and maintaining the way station. During the winter months Latimer would do a lot of reading – the *National Police Gazette* became his favorite magazine. Then, a few months after the end of the war, Ramble took sick. He passed away from pneumonia and Latimer was left on his own. Twenty-three and weary of working at the same job and never able to travel, Latimer sought new employment.

Having earned a reputation as a man who did the job and could also handle himself, he started riding shotgun and did some relief driving for the express and stagecoach company. He quickly proved his worth by defending the company's money and passengers whenever road agents attempted to rob the stage. His prowess with a gun again proved useful when a handful of renegade Indians tried to stop the stage. The company recognized his special abilities and began using him to protect shipments of gold or when a lot of cash was being moved. It wasn't something

Latimer wanted to do for the rest of his life, but it earned him better than average pay until something else came along.

CHAPTER TWO

Constance stormed in to confront her father at his Merchant's Bank office. He happened to be alone, so she closed the door behind her.

'Did you read the telegram I left on your desk?' she asked breathlessly.

Lionel Dewitt stroked his perfectly trimmed moustache, a habit of his whenever he was anxious or deeply concerned.

'Preposterous!' he declared. 'How could Sheldon have gotten into such a mess? Why weren't we notified by the proper authorities right away?'

'It's a territorial jail at Baxterville, Wyoming. The message appears to have been sent anonymously. It's possible the people there are afraid of the local law. The fact is, Sheldon is going to be tried for murder. He might be sentenced to hang!'

'I'll contact the attorney general and have him put a stop to it,' Lionel promised.

'Wyoming was only declared a territory a few months ago. What if those people don't recognize his authority?' lamented Constance. 'We can't sit by and let this happen.'

'I don't know what else we can do, daughter.'

Constance fumed and paced about the room, wringing her hands as ideas flashed through her mind. 'We must stop this. He's your only son left who. . . .' She stopped that argument and changed her approach. 'I'll go to Baxterville myself and put an end to this miscarriage of justice.'

'You don't have a background in law or any legal authority,' Lionel said. 'What can you possibly hope to do?'

'I can make sure Sheldon doesn't get railroaded to the gallows,' Constance declared. 'This has to be a mistake.'

'You can't make a trip all that way alone,' Lionel argued. 'And I can't leave the bank for an extended period of time. We've got our entire future at stake.'

'I'll hire a couple of men to take with me, men who aren't afraid of some backwoods lawman, whose only authority was granted to him by a handful of crooks.'

'Perhaps I can find a lawyer to send with you?'

'There isn't any time,' Constance answered firmly. 'All I need is the money to make the trip and pay for the help.'

'Take Simms with you. He can act as your chaperone

and be there if you run in to some financial difficulty,' Lionel outlined, speaking of the mild-mannered vice-president of the bank. 'But what about the legality of this? How do you propose to stop them from convicting Sheldon?'

'I'm sure he isn't guilty, Father. I'll find the highest authority in the territory to stand with me. We'll force them to move the trial to a neutral city or some place where we can get a real judge.'

'I'll contact the governor and ask for his help. I'm sure we can delay the trial for a few weeks.' He uttered a grunt of disgust. 'I didn't know Sheldon was going all the way to Wyoming and the Dakotas. What on earth was he doing so far from home?'

'You know Sheldon. He bragged to me that he was going on an extended hunting expedition. He wanted to bag a couple trophies for his office.'

'Office?' Lionel's brows crested high on his forehead. 'What office?'

'When we are ready to start another bank. He said you promised you would make him a bank president.'

'That could be years from now,' Lionel jeered. 'I told him he would have to learn the ropes and put in a lot of work first.'

'Well, you know Sheldon. A lot of work to him is getting up before noon and dressing himself. Anything more than that and he is worn out for a week.'

15

'All right, all right. You hire a couple of body-guards to go with you and I'll speak to Simms. Next, I'll put together some money and write out a couple of bank drafts you can use as you need the cash. However,' he eyed her with a skeptical gaze, 'be sure you hire trustworthy men. I'll worry myself sick if you end up wandering clear across the country with a pair of unsavory saddle bums.'

'Whatever you say, Father,' Constance promised, while not meeting his intense scrutiny. 'I'll be fine.'

Konrad Ellington had stopped at Broken Spoke, Wyoming, to visit his lady friend. Amber Walters, a widow in her early thirties, ran a ladies' dry goods store, mostly dress-material, fixings, threads, yarn and such. But her kids had been underfoot, so he hadn't had much time alone with her. His idea had been to wait until closing and hope she could find someone to watch the children for a couple hours. He wanted to talk about their future in private. At least, that had been his plan.

The stage arrived and he paused to watch. A lady stepped down from the coach, smartly dressed, with dark, raven-black hair pulled back in a severe bun at the back of her head. The sunhat she wore was quite stylish for this part of the country, and her entire outfit was more fashionable than most. The dress had a tunic-style bodice, which extended down to serve as an overskirt, although it was unbuttoned from the ankles to above the knees, revealing a ruffled white underskirt. Obviously, she preferred freedom of movement for riding in a cramped coach or walking. Just now her entire ensemble was covered with a thin layer of dust from the stage ride.

Mitt McGee, an acquaintance of Konrad's from previous visits to Broken Spoke, had been driving the stage. He left the team and proceeded to accompany the woman directly over to where Konrad was sitting on a porch chair, in front of the town pharmacy.

'Hey, Marshal,' McGee greeted him. 'Glad we finally caught up with you.'

'You've been looking for me?'

'Heard you were up this way visiting a friend.' McGee flashed a salacious wink. 'The lady here was keen on finding you.' With a shrug, 'Reckon it's because you are about the only real lawman we have in Wyoming, other than for a local badge here or there at a couple of the larger towns.'

Konrad smiled and asked, 'How's the family? You keeping a roof over the heads of your wife and your brood?'

'It keeps me busy,' McGee replied. 'I never expected to ever marry, let alone end up with a passel of young'uns.'

'You need to transfer to driving stage on longer runs, so you aren't home so much.'

McGee laughed. 'You're about five kids too late with that advice.'

Konrad chuckled at the remark, though he noticed the woman's gaze had grown cooler with impatience during the friendly exchange between him and McGee. He reluctantly got down to addressing her problem.

'I'm Konrad Ellington, US Marshal for Wyoming Territory . . . along with Colorado and a share of the Dakotas,' he explained to the woman. 'What can I do for you?'

'I am Constance Dewitt, Marshal.' Her tone was brusque. 'And I sought you out to acquire your help in securing the release of my brother, Sheldon. He has been falsely incarcerated by a corrupt judge and other villainous men who masquerade as the law over at Baxterville.'

'You say he's in jail?'

'Yes, with a charge of murder hanging over his head.'

McGee remarked to Konrad, 'Sam Gundy drives stage and makes the run from Rimrock to Baxterville and back twice a week. You ever been up that way?'

'No, but I do know it's over near the Montana-Wyoming border,' replied Konrad. 'I've heard a story or two about the town from a couple Canadian buffalo hunters I met at Laramie some time back.'

'They are charging my brother for a murder he didn't commit. If they find him guilty, they may very well hang him. My father has contacted the territorial governor and he promised to have them to delay the trial, but he won't intervene as to the handling of the case. I doubt there is a single honest-to-goodness judge in all of Wyoming.'

'Sam told me they had a city sheriff and a judge,' McGee jumped in. 'It's a fair-sized town, located in a valley that lies betwixt two mountain ranges. They get a lot of travelers going through to the Dakotas or Montana.'

'Do you have any proof of your brother's innocence?' Konrad asked the lady.

'I know Shelly is not a killer,' she stated piously.

He frowned. 'The word of a sister is hardly grounds for a judge to dismiss a murder case.'

'My father is Lionel Washington Dewitt. He is sole owner of the Merchant's Bank of St Louis. My brother didn't serve during the war and has only fired a gun when out hunting for game. He's about as docile as an earthworm and has never engaged in so much as a bout of fisticuffs in his life.'

'With your father being such a prominent citizen, why didn't he send a lawyer to try and win your brother's freedom?'

'Because we're talking about a hostile town with its own judge and rules. A man without a certain singular authority is not going to do any good.'

Konrad considered her argument, then observed, 'I'm surprised your father allowed you to travel all this way alone.'

She made a face. 'I began with one of our bank's

vice-presidents and two hired men,' she clarified.
'The smoke from the train caused the vice-president
to cough and hack like a man dying of consumption.
He feared the dust from a stagecoach would kill him.
Plus he had warm butter for a backbone and con-
stantly whined about every little discomfort.'
Constance sighed. 'I left him to catch the return
train at Fort Kearny.'

'And your hired men?'

'I spied an unsavory-looking gentleman talking to
them at the train station. I'm not sure what was discussed. However, when we picked up my luggage to
transfer it to the stage depot, the two employees
insisted that I more than double their pay. I refused
to pay such an extortionate amount and fired them
both.' She took a breath and levelled her gaze upon
Konrad. 'It was then that I decided to seek out the
law. The man at the telegraph station said you were
here in Broken Spoke, so I came to see you person-
ally. I need a man of influence – a man such as
yourself – to help me save my brother.'

'A US Marshal has a lot of responsibilities, but
investigating an arrest and conviction is not one of
them. We uphold the law and bring criminals to
justice; we serve warrants, settle disputes and handle
chores beyond the scope of local town or county
sheriffs. I don't have the jurisdiction to enter
Baxterville and demand the release of a prisoner.'

'But he was framed!'

'Why should they make up a charge against him?'

'I have no idea. Perhaps he saw something he shouldn't have, or maybe he inadvertently insulted someone. I don't know.'

McGee had not missed a word of the conversation. As Konrad pondered the problem he broke the uncomfortable silence.

'I wonder if Latimer could be of some help?'

Konrad eyed him thoughtfully. 'Dean Latimer? Did he arrive with you?'

McGee tipped his head in the direction of the coach. 'He rode shotgun for me on this trip. We were carrying a fair sum of money to deliver to the bank.' McGee pointed down the street. 'See? He's just finished getting the receipt for the transfer.'

Konrad paused to consider the young man. He had crossed trails with Latimer once or twice before and knew a little of his history. The man was quiet, yet capable, with a deadly aim and ice in his blood. He asked McGee what he thought.

'One thing I've learned about him, Konrad,' McGee replied, 'is that he is the most soft-spoken gent I ever met . . . considering the line of work he's in. Must have ridden with him a couple dozen times and I've never known him to lose his temper.'

This reinforced Konrad's opinion. 'I wonder if he might be a little too passive for a job like this?'

'Don't let his quiet and mannerly behavior fool you, Marshal. You remember the Eckland boys, over at Gillett, and the way they kept running roughshod over everyone in town?' He snapped his fingers. 'Latimer tamed them both without firing a shot. They are both serving time at Laramie prison as we speak.'

'I saw the Eckland names in a monthly crime report, but Latimer wasn't mentioned.'

'The local sheriff took credit for the arrest, but it was Latimer who took the two boys down.'

'I don't know.' The lady tossed in her two cents. 'I need someone who will stand up to corruption and isn't afraid of an authority figure. I don't know how much good a man will be if he can't assert himself.'

'Oh, he ain't afraid to assert himself,' McGee said. 'A coupla months back six bandits tried to stop the coach from Cheyenne whilst he was riding shotgun. He shot four of them and the stage kept right on rolling.'

'He might be just the man for the job, Miss Dewitt,' Konrad recommended. 'You can't go to a town where you think the judge and sheriff might be involved in something underhand and start throwing out accusations. To do any good, a man would have to be subtle, do some digging and see what is going on first.'

'My brother doesn't have a lot of time. They only agreed to hold up the trial for two weeks. That leaves me just four more days to get there and prove him innocent.'

'It's imperative we handle the situation properly, ma'am, and that means we have to do it legal and by the book. If you hire men for a jailbreak, then you're going to end up on the wrong side of the law yourself.'

She scowled at Konrad, but it was not evident in her voice. 'I understand how the judicial system works,' she said. 'You're asking me to be *subtle*, but my objective is to rescue my brother from a hangman's noose.'

'Everything depends on the circumstances – whether there is an organized conspiracy or maybe just an honest mistake. As for what I can do, I can appoint Latimer to look into this on your behalf. However, if he finds no evidence to the contrary, and your brother is found guilty. . . .' He gave a resolute grunt. 'Then there wouldn't be a thing we could do to prevent the hanging.'

Constance maintained a rigid posture, but she did not argue. 'I'll concede you are interested in seeing justice done. When does the coach head for Baxterville?'

'This is the end of the run here at Broken Spoke,' McGee informed her. 'You'll have to return to Rimrock and take the stage to Baxterville.'

The lady did not hide her distress at the news. She had just come an extra sixty miles and now she would have to return. With a measure of defeat visible in her face, she asked: 'Is there a place in town for me to wash up before we leave?'

'This is only a short stop-over to change the horses,' McGee said, keeping his voice as gentle as possible. 'Once we make the return trip, you will be traveling on an independent stage line that runs twice each week between Baxterville and Rimrock. The good news is we will be back in time for you to get a night's sleep and still make the connection with that outgoing stage. Sam Gundy lives in Rimrock and drives the stage up and back. He's a good man.'

Constance groaned. 'I suppose there's little need to wash or change clothes.'

'You've time enough to eat,' McGee suggested. 'The Chinese cook at the saloon actually puts out the best meal in town.'

Konrad said, 'I'll introduce you to Latimer. If he is receptive to the idea, we can share a table with him and discuss our options while we eat. That will give you a chance to get to know him and decide whether or not this arrangement might suit your needs.'

CHAPTER THREE

Latimer hadn't spoken to the elegant female passenger on the trip from Rimrock. He had replaced the guard who had been on the run from Cheyenne, but McGee had been the one to check the lady's ticket and welcome her aboard. He wondered at the long conversation between McGee, the US marshal and the woman. When McGee waved to him to join them he experienced a sudden chill of apprehension – like the old saying about *having someone walk over your grave.*

As he approached the trio he touched the brim of his hat in a salutatory gesture. 'Miss.' He spoke to the lady first and then to the lawman. 'Marshal . . . Ellington, isn't it?'

'Konrad Ellington, that's right. And I know a little about you too, Mr Dean Latimer,' the marshal responded.

McGee jumped into the conversation to explain

the lady's mission and asked if he would be willing to help. Latimer took a moment to study the woman. She sported a stern, no-nonsense countenance and studied him with a cool perusal. Her features were quite delicate and fair, with ink black hair to accent the buffed ivory of her complexion. She had erect posture and was maybe four or five inches shorter than his own five-foot-ten-inch frame. The fabric of her clothing and hat appeared expensive. As for the name, Dewitt, he didn't recognize it, but then he never paid much attention to higher class social types.

'Well?' she asked impatiently, boring into him with the prettiest chocolate-colored eyes he'd ever seen.

'That explains why you're toting a Saratoga,' he evaded her question. 'We're a long way from St Louis.'

'I needed a sizeable trunk so I could change clothes during the many days of travel.'

Latimer looked at the marshal. 'What's your part in this?'

'I've a mind to deputize you,' Konrad answered. 'What would you think of that?'

'To do what exactly?'

A new look entered the woman's eyes as she measured him more closely and she burst forth, 'To prevent my brother from being hanged, of course!'

'Even if I pinned on a badge, I can only do what I can do, miss,' he answered honestly. 'If the proof of his guilt is beyond doubt. I won't break the law.'

She squared her shoulders adamantly. 'He was framed. I'm sure of it.'

'The man is your brother. I wouldn't think you much of a sister if you didn't believe in his innocence.'

'What is your answer?' The lady pressed for a decision. 'I'll pay you a hundred dollars a week and a five-hundred dollar bonus the day you get my brother out of this terrible situation.'

McGee whistled. 'Maybe I should have volunteered for the job.'

'That's downright extravagant,' was Latimer's reply.

'And a lot more than you will earn as my deputy,' Konrad contributed.

Latimer frowned, wondering if this was a way to earn a pile of money or just the shortest route to getting himself killed.

'How about you join the lady and me for a meal and we can hash over a few details?' Konrad invited him. 'I'll explain the role I expect from a deputy.' He directed those words to Dean, then looked at Constance. 'And you can add what you know about your brother's situation.'

'That idea has merit; I'm quite famished,' Miss Dewitt said, allowing a slight smile of appreciation to flatter her features.

'Works for me,' Latimer agreed. A meal was on his

list of to-do things before the stage pulled out, anyway.

'What are you doing about this?' Janus Poe grilled the town sheriff, waving the telegraph message wildly about in his hand. 'Didn't you find out who this guy was before you arrested him?'

Sheriff Milburn's shoulders drooped ignominiously, but his voice was defensive. 'Who could have known Dewitt had a father with that much clout?'

Janus swore. 'This is the last thing we need right now. With Graham out of the picture everything was taken care of. Now we are backed in a corner.'

'Don't get your nose twisted out of shape, Judge,' Milburn soothed Janus's ire, pulling a similar piece of paper from his shirt pocket. 'Soon as we learned about Dewitt's sister coming, I sent Bo Janks to intercept her at the train station. I got this message back from him.' With a sneer, 'Bo made a deal and bought off the two hired guns the lady arrived with.'

'What?'

'Seems they were the kind of men who were receptive to a plan to make a lot more money. After Bo talked to them, they demanded more money for the job and the gal fired them both.'

Janus was alert now. 'Then she has no help?'

Milburn grinned. 'I told you I would take care of things. Bo is going to pull a little job with those two newly unemployed bodyguards. Remember, Judge, that gal is worth a lot of money.'

'We can't underestimate Dewitt's father. He managed to get the governor to intervene and postpone the trial for two weeks.'

'The problem is solved,' Milburn assured him confidently. 'Bo is going to prevent the woman from showing up, and make a pile of money doing it.'

Janus arched his brows in disbelief. 'You're going to kidnap the Dewitt woman and demand ransom?'

'Kidnap and ransom are crude and unsavory terms,' Milburn corrected. 'I prefer to think of it as delaying the lady's arrival and charging her father a fat fee for looking after her for a few days. I told Bo to ask for five thousand dollars for her safe return.'

'A kidnapping could lead the law to us.'

'There isn't enough law in this territory to stop a runaway turtle.' Milburn waved a hand as if to brush away a pesky fly. 'The thing is, while old man Dewitt is busy paying for the return of his daughter, we will have the trial, convict a murderer, and his boy will be hanged and buried before his sister can arrive.'

Janus mopped his damp brow as nervous perspiration popped up on his forehead. 'I begin to regret all of this,' he whined. 'Murder. Now kidnapping. I didn't think—'

'And you don't have to start thinking now!' Milburn snapped, cutting off his sentence. 'I've got the plan as to how we can own this town. When the railroad runs a spur north to Montana we will be rich beyond our dreams.'

The judge allowed a compliant nod, but the worry lines deepened across his beaded brow. He'd never thought the path to the riches Milburn promised would become so steep and treacherous.

Latimer rode shotgun on the return trip to Rimrock. Constance got a room at a hotel for the night while Latimer bunked at the sleeping quarters provided for drivers above the express office. The stage to Baxterville didn't leave until morning, so it gave the lady and Latimer time to clean up and get a full night's sleep.

Constance arrived at the express office shortly after the stage was parked out front. Taking stock of the man called Latimer, she admitted to herself that he looked much better in a dark suit and a felt, flat-crowned hat. Even his boots were polished and, other than wearing a gun on his hip, he looked very much a proper gentleman. Clean-shaven, with hair moderately shorn, and very tanned from being exposed to the weather year around, he wasn't altogether unattractive. He was talking to the stage driver as she approached, the man named Sam Gundy. Obviously the two of them had known each other for several years, as they spoke of old times and someone named Ramble.

Soon as the mail, luggage and express items were loaded, Sam climbed up to take his position as the driver. This time Latimer held the door for Constance and followed her inside the coach.

The ride started with a lurch and they were on their way to Baxterville. Along the route Latimer kept to himself and seldom offered a word. Constance talked some and he listened politely, occasionally gave a nod of agreement or understanding, but added little to the discussion. She began to wonder if Latimer was uncomfortable at the idea of working for a woman.

'You are not much for conversation, are you?' she asked, after he had answered a half-dozen questions with single word replies.

'No, miss,' he said.

'Don't you have questions about my brother? Aren't you concerned as to why I believe he is innocent? How do you know he didn't commit the crime for which he has been sentenced?'

'You seem sincere about the question of his guilt. I reckon we'll be able to prove him innocent if that's the case.'

'How can we prove it?'

'Won't know that until we hear his side of the story,' was Latimer's reply. Then he fell to silence until Constance became frustrated.

'So is it me?' she demanded to know. 'Are you reserved or introverted because you haven't spent much time around an educated lady – is that your problem?'

'What does that there introvert thing mean?' he asked her respectfully.

She remained exasperated, but kept her poise. 'I'm wondering, Mr Latimer, if you're afraid of me. I am curious as to how you think we should proceed. Are you working on a plan?' She asked the questions with some impatience. 'Have you even given the job ahead some consideration?'

'Uh, which question would you like me to answer?'

'All of them!' she snapped. 'I've been worried sick about my brother. He must be frightened and he's all alone. He's never been in trouble with the law. Shelly doesn't even drink to excess.'

'Perhaps you should return to Rimrock,' Latimer suggested. 'You could stay in a hotel and would have decent places to eat and shop. I can look over the situation in Baxterville and see what can be done for your bother.'

'That is totally unacceptable.' She snipped off the words. 'I'm Shelly's sister and I am going to protest against his incarceration and this farcical trial most vociferously.'

Latimer frowned at her literary display. He had read some of the words she used but he'd never heard them spoken. He was about to remark about how well educated she must be when the stage lurched and suddenly began to slow down.

'Bandits!' the driver called back to them.

'Easy, Sam,' Latimer advised him through the

window. 'Just do what they say.'

Three masked men on horseback appeared outside the window, keeping pace as the stage's speed decreased. Latimer noticed that one was leading a saddled horse with no rider. The guy nearest the coach held a rifle pointed up at Sam. The other two had their pistols out.

'You carrying a lot of money?' Latimer asked her quietly.

'Quite a lot actually . . . in my purse.'

He didn't ask permission, but quickly reached over and opened the bag. He removed a wad of bills and peeled off a couple. Those he put back and handed the rest to her.

'Stick that inside your blouse,' he told her. 'Hurry.'

The stage rolled slowly to a complete stop and one of the men dismounted and aimed his gun at the coach. 'You in the stage,' he ordered. 'Outside where we can see you!'

Constance pulled the collar away from her neck and pushed the money down between her breasts. Latimer removed the thong from his Remington New Model Army revolver and opened the door, moving slowly, so the lady had time to smooth her clothing back into place. He got out, then waited to lend her a hand. She paused to look at the hold-up men before stepping down, then gasped.

Latimer glanced at her face and saw a flash of surprise. Ducking her head as she climbed down, she whispered, 'I recognize the men on horses – they are the two I fired!'

'Stop flapping your yap, woman!' the man on the ground snarled.

'We ain't carrying no strongbox,' Sam told the three men. 'There's no money being transferred from Rimrock to the bank in Baxterville on this run. Got nothing but a little mail and a package or two.'

'Shut your pie-hole, driver!' the bandit with the rifle warned Sam.

'What is it you want?' Latimer asked, lifting his hands to shoulder level while quickly scanning the area for the fourth man. If they had a shooter hidden in the brush and covering the hold-up, any resistance would mean a quick death.

'You and the driver can continue on your way, bucko,' the man standing a few away announced haughtily. 'We only want the woman. She goes with us!'

CHAPTER FOUR

'What are you talking about?' Sam asked from atop the stage. 'You boys ain't fools enough to kidnap a woman?'

'I've got a letter explaining how things will be,' the masked man growled, patting his pocket with his free hand. 'You want to end up dead, you keep yapping.'

Latimer sized up the three men and made a quick decision. 'I think you boys made a mistake.'

His comment caused the two men with handguns to point them menacingly in his direction. 'What I mean is,' Latimer quickly explained, 'you brought the wrong kind of saddle. This here is a proper lady. I doubt she's ever ridden astride a horse in her life. You should have gotten a side-saddle rig for her.'

'She'll take what we brung,' the one holding the extra horse barked.

Latimer lowered both hands to chest level, palms outward, making a gesture that he was only trying to help. 'There is an easy way to solve the problem,' he clarified.

The statement caused the trio to display curiosity. The man on the ground asked, 'What way are you talking about?'

'It's a simple trick,' Latimer said, intently awaiting the right moment. 'You remove the stirrup on the right side of the horse and secure the strap to the saddle horn. That puts both stirrups on the same side of the saddle.'

The bandit with the spare horse looked at the extra mount, studying how such a silly-sounding idea could work. In that single moment, the other two outlaws also focused their attention on the spare horse and saddle. The instant all three were looking away from Latimer, he grabbed his gun.

The rider with the rifle sensed movement, but he had to shift his body round to bring his carbine to bear on Latimer. He did manage a cry of warning . . . too late!

Latimer fired virtually point blank into the nearest man and stepped in front of Constance to shield her with his body. The shot from his pistol caused the horses to balk, jump and dance about. Before the one with the rifle could control his mount and align a shot, Latimer put a slug through his chest. The third man was battling three spooked horses – his own, his pal's, who was on the ground, and the extra mount. He managed to get them under control enough to fire a hasty shot in Latimer's direction.

The bullet struck the side of the coach as Latimer pulled the trigger on his gun. He scored a hit, but the slug hit the man too low. It buckled the would-be kidnapper over his saddle, but it didn't put him out of the fight. He stayed aboard his skittish mount and, with a mighty effort, he raised his pistol to try and shoot again.

Latimer had no choice but to finish him off. This time his deadly aim knocked the man out of the saddle. He toppled to the ground in a heap and lay still.

Quickly assessing each of the three men, Latimer discovered two were already dead and the last one, who had been on the ground when shot, didn't have long. Kneeling at his side, Latimer pulled down the road agent's mask.

'Who sent you, fella?' he asked gently. 'Who's the man responsible for my being forced to kill you and your friends?'

The man grimaced with pain, rolled his head back and forth and coughed. A sigh of death escaped his lips, his sightless eyes stared back at Latimer, and the life was gone from his body.

Constance came to stand by Latimer's side. She was visibly shaken by the sudden explosion of gunfire and death, but she mustered a measure of bravado. 'That's the man who met my two hired men at the train station.'

Sam set the coach brake and climbed down to join Latimer and Constance.

'You know him?' Latimer asked.

'I've seen him around Baxterville a time or two, but don't rightly know his name.' Sam bent over to pluck the envelope from the dead man's pocket. Peeling it open he snorted.

'Yep, this here is a demand for five thousand dollars for the lady's safe return. These three coyotes was sure enough gonna take the gal with them.' He moved over and handed the note to Miss Dewitt.

Constance scanned the ransom demand and regarded Latimer with confusion. 'How could this man have known I would be on the train? And how did he manage to buy off my two hired men and turn them against me!'

Latimer deduced, 'Someone knew you were coming. This guy probably suggested to your men that they could all make some easy money by taking you for ransom. Didn't you say the pair were some-time bounty hunters?'

'Yes. It's why I assumed they would risk their necks for the high wages.'

'I'd guess this fellow figured the same way, except he offered them a better deal to betray you.'

The lady's pallor showed she was close to nausea from witnessing the deaths of three men, but she maintained a sturdy façade. Latimer rotated about to stand in front of her. Gently but firmly, he suggested she get back in the coach.

Constance nodded and obediently returned to the coach. Latimer followed along and gave her a hand as she climbed back inside, where she took her seat.

'Catch up the horses, Sam,' he instructed the driver, returning to the chore at hand. 'We'll tether the animals behind the stage.'

'Sure thing, Lat,' Sam replied. 'We can toss the bodies in the boot until we reach Baxterville. There's nothing back there but the lady's trunk and we can move it topside.'

'That should work,' Latimer said. Then, with a grim expression, 'I'm curious as to who will admit they know the mystery guy who recruited Miss Dewitt's hired men.'

The two of them worked together and had everything ready to go in a matter of minutes. Latimer thought about allowing the woman some time alone, but decided he had better ride with her. She might have questions, or concerns about continuing the journey.

Constance rode in silence for the next hour. She was obviously deep in thought and disturbed by the deadly event. Latimer allowed her to process what had taken place and passed the time by looking out of the window.

'You took on three men to protect me.' The woman's grave voice broke the lengthy silence. When he turned to look at her, she continued, 'You bravely stood between me and those potential kidnappers and fought them to their deaths.'

'I'm sorry that it was necessary,' Latimer responded.

The lady frowned. 'Necessary? You could have let those men take me; my father would have paid the ransom.'

Latimer hated to increase the woman's dismay, but he felt it necessary to be truthful. 'Those men would never have let you go,' he told her quietly. 'Once they got their money they would have had to kill you.'

'Why would they do that?'

'You recognized them – remember?' He clarified. 'Once they got you away from the stage they would surely have realized you knew who they were. Unless they wanted to be on the run for the rest of their lives they would have been forced to silence you for ever. You would have identified them.'

She comprehended his deduction and swallowed hard, as if to stifle a cry of realization. 'I . . . I didn't think about that.'

'It's why I couldn't let them take you,' Latimer reiterated. 'I had to risk trying to stop them.'

'But . . . but they had us under their guns and there were three of them!' Constance stared at him in a confounded amazement. 'How could you possibly think you could win a fight against such odds?'

'Actually, I didn't figure any of them would get off

a shot.' He sighed deeply, as if to apologize for his miscalculation. 'That last man could have hit you or me . . . maybe both of us.'

She gaped in disbelief. 'That's unbelievable! How could you possibly assume that none of them would have a chance to shoot back?'

'Three bandits,' Latimer outlined his logic. 'Two were still mounted and one of those two was holding a rifle.' Her brow furrowed with concentration as he went on. 'I took down the man on the ground first. I expected the gunshot would cause the horses to jump, or be spooked by the sudden noise, which they were. Next, the rifleman had to use both hands to fire, yet I turned my gun on him second. The reason for that is because he appeared to be an able man with a gun. Lastly, the third man was holding the reins of three horses, which meant he would have a hard time trying to control all of those animals and still get off a decent shot. Turns out, he did manage one round, but he didn't have time to aim. Before he could shoot a second time, I was able to end the fight.'

If Constance had not been bounced from going through a rut she would have sat stone still and simply stared at Latimer in wonder. He had taken only a few seconds to comprehend her dire situation, put the trio of kidnappers off guard with a diversion, then systematically eliminate them in a precise analytical order.

At her prolonged silence, Latimer cleared his throat. 'Besides,' he said seriously, 'Marshal Ellington entrusted your safety to me and you hired me to help win your brother's freedom. I was only doing the job both of you hired me to do.'

Her somber mood lightened and a slight smile tugged at the corners of her mouth. 'You are insightful, composed and chivalrous, Mr Latimer, much more than I expected.'

'Maybe I'm just a whole lot dumber,' he quipped.

She laughed, partly to vent some of the built-up adrenaline from the terror and turmoil of being nearly kidnapped. 'I believe you are the very man for whom I've been searching.'

Latimer grinned, 'Funny, but I never figured to hear a genuine lady say those words to me.'

Constance grew thoughtful for a moment, reflecting upon her declaration, then laughed again.

Judge Janus Poe marched into the office of Sheriff Morgan Milburn. Not wanting to say anything where the single prisoner could overhear, he motioned him to the doorway.

Milburn walked over to stand at his side, but Janus only pointed down the street.

Following the man's finger, Milburn about swallowed his teeth. It was the stage, parked in front of the express office. The elegant lady standing on the walk, awaiting the offloading of her luggage, had to be Constance Dewitt.

'It's not possible!' Milburn cried. 'Bo's wire said everything was going as planned. That meant he hired the two men who were supposed to be riding with her. Could that be another woman?'

'There's four horses tied on a lead rope behind the stage,' Janus hissed testily. 'And Hap overheard Sam telling Brinkerhoff they had three bodies in the boot – three dead would-be kidnappers!'

Milburn swore. 'What the devil went wrong? The gal should have been hidden away at Graham's old line shack by this time. We were supposed to send a wire demanding payment for the woman's return and all of us would have made a tidy sum for our troubles.'

'Well, it didn't turn out that way, did it!' Janus exclaimed. 'Do you see the man helping Sam with the luggage?' He let Milburn take a closer look and watched the scowl spread over his face.

'The man in the suit?' He muttered, 'He looks a bit like that stage guard . . . that Latimer fellow.'

Janus interjected hotly, 'It is!'

Milburn swore and stared even harder. 'It can't be! Latimer has never ridden guard for the trip up here. Ours is a private stage line. What the duce was he doing on board?'

'Does it matter?'

Milburn snorted his contempt. 'Well, we stick to the plan. We've got a solid case against Sheldon

Dewitt. Having his sister here is going to be a nuisance but it won't change the outcome.'

Janus tugged at his worn stovepipe hat. 'You had better find out why Latimer was on the stage and clean up this mess. Whatever you do, don't give him a reason to stick around.'

'I'll see to it,' Milburn promised.

'And, Sheriff,' Janus added, flashing a sarcastic sneer, 'make sure Miss Dewitt is taken care of. When this is over we don't want her father complaining that we didn't do everything according to the letter of the law.'

Milburn bobbed his head. 'Oh yeah, I'll see the lady has everything she asks for . . . except a "Not Guilty" verdict for her brother.'

CHAPTER FIVE

Sam was passing down the mail when he glanced up the street. He whispered to Latimer, 'Sheriff Milburn is coming.'

Latimer quickly turned to a rather slow-witted fellow – he wore a deputy's badge and was called Hap – who had been hanging around and asking questions.

'Do you know who this guy is, Hap?' he asked, indicating the one unknown bandit. 'Sam said he had seen him around town a time or two.'

'Sure,' Hap replied, showing a near-toothless grin. 'That there is Bo Janks.'

'Did he work for someone in town?'

Hap studied on it for a moment, as if it took time for his brain to process the question. 'I've known the sheriff to give him a job or two,' Hap admitted. 'You know, most often the kind of chore. . . .' Suddenly he went silent as the sheriff arrived.

45

'What's going on here, Hap?' Milburn's demand prevented the deputy from saying more. 'What about all these bodies?'

'Brung you three lowdown, rotten kidnappers, Sheriff.' Sam answered the question from atop the stage. 'They stopped us a few miles back and tried to take Miss Dewitt with them.' He cackled like a hen who's discovered the first egg in her nest. 'But them boys didn't count on Latimer being on board. He nailed all three of them like boards on a picket fence, and there they be . . . all laid out in a row.'

'Kidnappers, you say?'

'Yep,' Sam replied. 'That polecat at Hap's feet has a ransom note. We read it and put it back in his pocket for you. These lowlife scum was figuring to trade the lady's freedom for five thousand dollars.'

Hap put a boot to the man on the ground and tipped his head towards Milburn. 'It's Bo Janks, Sheriff. I don't know the other two, but the woman said she hired them back in St Louis. Then, when it came time to leave the train, the two men asked for more money and she cut 'em loose.'

'So they talked Bo into helping them kidnap the woman from the stage,' Milburn surmised. 'Bo always was the kind of man who was looking to make easy money.'

Hap laughed. 'He done hitched his wagon to a dead horse, stopping a stage with Latimer aboard.'

The sheriff scowled at Latimer. 'How did you

happen to be on the stage? Baxterville provides its own guards when they are needed for stage runs.'

'I hired on with Miss Dewitt,' Latimer replied. 'She needed an attorney for her brother, so I came along to see he gets a fair trial.'

'Attorney?' Milburn laughed at the absurdity. 'You ain't no attorney.'

Latimer didn't even blink. 'Beg to differ with you, Sheriff, but anyone can represent an accused man, so long as that man agrees to let him act on his behalf.'

Constance had moved close enough to overhear the exchange. Her eyes widened in surprise at Latimer's assertion, but she didn't speak up to contradict him. Instead, she stepped over to his side.

'I should like to visit my brother as soon as possible.' She addressed the sheriff.

Milburn took a moment to size her up, his eyes passing fleetingly over her from hat to shoes before resting on her determined face. He tipped his head affirmatively.

'Certainly, Miss Dewitt. It's fortunate you got here as soon as you did. The judge has this case scheduled for the day after tomorrow.'

'We will want to speak to my client privately,' Latimer informed Milburn.

'Well, I don't know if that will be possible. The man is—'

'It's the law,' Latimer was abrupt. 'You have no choice in the matter, but I wanted to give you the opportunity to prove you run an honest town.'

The muscles of Milburn's jaw tightened but he contained his anger and muttered, 'Of course. I am always willing to adhere to the letter of the law. Perhaps the lady here would prefer to freshen up first? It's a long dusty road between here and Rimrock.'

'That's very thoughtful of you, Sheriff,' Constance responded.

Milburn rubbed his chin and gazed at Latimer with a guarded expression. 'I'm curious as to how you two ended up together.'

Constance started to speak, but Latimer blocked her by asking: 'Who did Bo Janks work for in town?' He continued at once with a more pointed accusation. 'Someone must have known Miss Dewitt was going to be on the stage. Whoever it is might have sent Bo on a mission to kidnap her. You ought to look into that, Sheriff.'

'I don't need you to tell me my job!' Milburn snapped.

Latimer handed him a sheet of paper. 'This is the information on the other two men who were with Janks. Miss Dewitt has listed what she knew about them.'

The sheriff stared at the paper. 'Bounty hunters?'

'I erred in judgement by hiring the pair,' Constance told him. 'I was desperate and in a hurry. They were the only men I could find on short notice.'

'Hap,' Milburn directed, 'get these three bodies over to Doc's place so they can be buried quick and proper.'

'Where can we get the best room for a lady?' Latimer asked, as the deputy began to call out to some men to lend a hand with the outlaws.

Milburn gestured across the street. 'The hotel next to the general store. They offer baths and a barber.'

'Thank you, Sheriff. After Miss Dewitt is settled in we will be over to speak to her brother.'

'Yeah, all right.'

Latimer took charge of the lady's large Saratoga and pulled the trunk up to haul on his back. Then he and Constance started off toward the hotel. She walked at his side and regarded him with a curious look.

'You are going to hide the fact that you are a deputy US marshal and instead act as a defence attorney?' She was obviously confused by his declaration to the sheriff. 'When did we agree that an elaborate subterfuge was the best way to approach this situation?'

'I need to talk to your brother,' Latimer advised her. 'Once we know what kind of case they have against him, I can tell you whether or not we will need a real lawyer.'

'All right,' she acquiesced without further questions. 'You've proved yourself to be a man who thinks and acts with purpose. I will trust you to decide how best to proceed.'

Her confidence instilled a spark of pride in Latimer. 'I'll try not to disappoint you, Miss Dewitt,' he told her.

'It's crazy!' Sheldon cried, his knuckles white from gripping the cell bars. 'I didn't do anything. I was in bed asleep.'

Latimer surveyed the man. Although he was wearing an expensive suit, it was dirty and wrinkled from his being confined in a jail cell. His hair was unkempt, but had been barbered a few weeks past. Sheldon's complexion was pale, almost ashen, but his eyes were red from lack of sleep, and deep worry lines creased his forehead.

'Tell us exactly how you ended up being charged with murder,' Latimer encouraged the man. 'Don't leave anything out.'

Sheldon was trembling as if he were suffering from the cold. Constance opened her purse and removed the makings for a cigarette.

'I thought you might need this,' she said.

'Oh, you really are the greatest sister in the world,' Sheldon said enthusiastically. 'Could you roll it for me?' he asked. 'I'm so shaky I'd probably spill the makings all over the floor.'

Constance handed the tobacco sack and paper to Latimer. Although Latimer didn't smoke often, he quickly rolled a smoke and soon Sheldon was puffing away like a man who's been given a cup of water when dying of thirst.

'He can't live without his cigarettes,' Constance explained. 'Father says he is dependent on tobacco.' With a sigh, 'And I have to agree.'

'Seen that a few times,' Latimer said. 'I've known some men who would trade their horse or guns for a smoke or chaw of tobacco.'

Once his nerves had settled Sheldon explained what had happened on the night everything went wrong. He had drunk a couple beers at Pine's Palace, one of the three saloons in town, and was asking around to find a good hunting guide. Most of the companies who hosted hunts comprised several men, with wagons and cooks, tents and transportation all combined. He wanted to try his luck with just one man: a scout or hunter who knew where to find prize game.

Having no luck at finding such a man, he returned to the hotel and went to bed. About an hour later he thought he heard a gunshot. With a saloon only a couple doors down, he didn't give it a thought, until the sheriff and his deputy burst in and arrested him for the murder of Amble Graham, a horse rancher who lived a short way from town.

'Did you know this Graham fellow?' Latimer asked.

'We talked for a few minutes at the saloon that

night. He agreed to rent me the horses I would need when I was ready to leave for the hunt. I certainly didn't have any grudge against him.'

'Why did they suspect you?'

'The banker, a man named Bellows, said he saw me and Graham arguing in the alleyway next to the saloon. He claims I pulled a gun and shot Graham, then tossed the pistol away and left him to die.'

'He actually saw the murder?'

'That's what he said,' Sheldon replied.

'He's a man I will need to talk to,' Latimer said.

'I don't know what. . . .' Sheldon began, but Latimer held up a hand to stop him from speaking.

Milburn had been outside the building, but he entered unobtrusively and took a seat at his desk. Maybe nothing . . . yet it was possible the guy intended to overhear what was being said.

'Let me see your hands,' Latimer requested of Sheldon. After a quick inspection, he noticed a callus on Sheldon's left thumb and grinned. 'Play the guitar, do you?'

Sheldon laughed. 'I did a lot of picking tunes when I was back home. I've been wishing I had brought my guitar with me so I could kill the time. The hours really drag by being locked up in this cell.'

'Do you usually carry a gun?'

'I travel with my hunting rifle, a Winchester, but I don't own a handgun.'

'You said the banker saw you toss your gun after

shooting Graham. Did they recover the weapon?'

'Yes. It's a Colt Model Navy. The sheriff has it locked away for evidence.' Sheldon crossed his heart. 'I swear to you, Mr Latimer, I've never fired a gun like that before in my life.'

Latimer turned to face Constance. She had been true to her word in letting him do all of the questioning. Deep concern shone in her enticingly beautiful dark eyes as she awaited his conclusions.

'It's getting late,' he said. 'I'm going to have supper with Sam and see that those three outlaws have been put in the ground. I also need to send a wire to the US marshal's office and inform them about the attempted kidnapping. You get some rest and we'll get together in the morning.'

Rather than allow him to leave, Constance grabbed him by the arm. 'What do you think about Shelly's case?'

Latimer glanced at the sheriff. He appeared to be ignoring them, intently reading a Wanted notice. Instead of answering directly Latimer winked at her. After a short pause he used a grave tone of voice and said, 'It doesn't sound good, Miss Dewitt, but we will do what we can.'

Constance picked up on his gesture of reassurance, as well as his distrust of the sheriff. As Latimer left the office, she took her brother's hand between her own and gave it a squeeze.

'We'll get through this, Shelly,' she said. 'I'm sure

the truth will come out.'

'Wish I shared your optimism, Sis. I really got myself in a mess this time, and all because I wanted to impress Dad with a couple of trophies.'

'Hard work is all that impresses Father. You should have learned that by now.'

'Get me out of this and I'll work sixteen hours a day to prove I'm worthy to be his son.'

'Let's not be excessive,' she replied. 'Ten hours a day ought to suffice.'

Milburn stuck Hap at the jail and went to visit with Janus. He told him about Latimer taking on the role of defence lawyer for Dewitt. He also outlined the botched attempt by Bo Janks and the two hired men to kidnap the woman.

'It would seem the stories we've heard about Latimer are true,' the judge said woefully. 'Who would have thought he could kill three men . . . after they had him covered with their own guns.'

'He was asking who might have sent Bo to meet the train.' Milburn stiffened his jaw to control his anger. 'And he is going to talk to Bellows.'

'Francis knows what he has to do.' Janus dismissed his fears. 'He won't give away anything.'

'That Latimer might cause us trouble. We had this planned so we wouldn't have anyone questioning Bellows's testimony. That woman should have never arrived.'

'It's done now, Sheriff. We will have to deal with it.'

Milburn rubbed his chin thoughtfully. 'Maybe if we gave Latimer and the woman something more to worry about it might distract them from a proper investigation.'

'What are you thinking?'

'Cowlick and Marco are in town. Both of them worked with Bo on occasion. They might enjoy a little payback.'

Janus displayed alarm. 'They can't back-shoot Latimer! We would have the US marshal up here in a heartbeat.'

'I was thinking more of a diversion, something to keep him occupied,' Milburn replied. 'A couple broken bones would slow down anything Latimer had in mind, and both Cowlick and Marco are rough and tumble fighters. You remember Cowlick gouged that hunter's eye out last year.' He grunted in disgust. 'He bragged to me it was the third man he had blinded on one side.'

'Cowlick's an animal,' Janus agreed. Still concerned over the plan, he said, 'I'm not sure how that would play out, those two picking a fight with Latimer.'

Milburn grinned. 'They won't be the ones starting the fight. I've an idea to let Latimer be the one who does that.'

Janus went along. 'All right, Sheriff. Do what you can to dissuade Dewitt's lawyer without forcing me to delay the trial. We want this over and done with as soon as possible.'

'Leave it to me, Judge. I'll take care of everything.'

The next morning Latimer met Constance for breakfast and discussed the plan for the day. She had some personal things to attend to and Latimer was eager to start his investigation. They parted company after the meal and he headed over to talk to the banker and lone witness, Francis Bellows.

Latimer located the man in his office at the bank. Francis was thin enough to have been living on a steady diet of prunes and water. He had something of a hook nose and a couple of protruding teeth. Latimer comprehended his pompous demeanor at once – skinny, homely kid, probably teased all his life, but now he had money and position, which he used to get even with society.

Latimer extended a hand as he introduced himself. Francis reluctantly accepted it in a limp shake. Then Latimer explained he was going to act as Sheldon's attorney and wanted to hear about the night of the murder.

'I've known a few lawyers; you won't trick me when I testify,' Francis said importantly with a sniff. 'I deal with all kinds of people and have learned how to interpret their artifices.'

Latimer wasn't sure what an *artifice* was, but he mustered up a look of being impressed. 'I can see you're no fool, Mr Bellows. However, I am hoping to gain a little sympathy from the court for my client.' He gave a heave of his shoulders. 'It seems it is about his only chance to escape a noose.'

'That will be a considerable chore,' Francis gloated. 'After all, it was cold-blooded murder.'

'Did you hear what the two men were fighting about?'

'No, but it was the argument that caught my attention, you know, their loud and angry exchange.'

'And you actually saw Mr Dewitt pull a gun and shoot Mr Graham?' At the banker's nod Latimer queried, 'How close was he to Mr Graham?'

'Less than three feet,' Francis proclaimed. 'He was close enough that he couldn't miss.' With a snort of contempt, 'Almost put the gun up against the man's chest when he pulled the trigger.'

'You've no doubt it was Mr Dewitt? I mean, wasn't it dark in the alley?'

'Nope. I got me a clear look at his clothes and face. It was him all right.'

'Then, after Mr Dewitt shot the man, he simply threw the gun down?'

Francis rose to his feet and mimicked what he had seen. He pretended to pull a gun from his waistband, reached out with a pointed finger to represent the gun and said 'Bang!'. Then he went through the motion of tossing the pistol at the mortally wounded victim's feet. 'That's just how it happened.'

Latimer displayed a grim resolve, as if accepting that Dewitt's situation was hopeless. 'Thank you for your time, Mr Bellows. I appreciate your talking to me.'

Francis returned to the work on his desk and, in a sign of dismissal, he said, 'No trouble at all, Mr Latimer. I'll see you at the trial tomorrow.'

As Latimer was busy interviewing people, Constance dropped off her traveling clothes at a laundry and ordered a bath. She was pleasantly surprised to find that the bathhouse had a woman employee who shampooed, cut and styled ladies' hair. She took advantage of the opportunity, wanting to look as presentable as possible for the upcoming trial. The entire ordeal took the better part of the morning. When she left the bath-and-barber part of the hotel, she felt refreshed and clean for the first time since she had left home.

'Cast your blinkers at the new heifer in town, Cowlick.' A heckling voice caused Constance to cringe. Her way was suddenly blocked by two dirty, unsavory-looking men. Neither of them appeared to have shaved or bathed in weeks, both were wearing dirty trousers held up by wide suspenders, and cotton work-shirts. They wore guns in holsters on thick leather belts with filled ammunition loops.

'Bet this here is the new gal hired to work at Pine's Palace,' one of the men deduced, a sneer curling his thick lips.

' 'Course she is, Marco,' the other confirmed. 'Look at them fancy rags she's a-wearing.'

'Yehaw!' Marco shouted, clapping his hands enthusiastically. 'You and me is gonna be first to taste her charms, Cowlick. Yes siree, you and me will sure have us some fun.'

Constance hid her immediate fear and put a hard look on the two louses. 'I am not one of the squalid entertainers who works at the drinking emporium, gentlemen. Please allow me to pass.'

'Squalid?' Cowlick repeated. 'Ain't that one of them things from the ocean that's got lots of legs?'

Constance frowned. 'As you obviously understand only the most basic colloquial English, I shall explain. I do not work at any saloon or dancehall, nor do I fraternize with drunken rowdies.'

'You hear that?' Marco jeered. 'She don't frater herself with your kind.'

'Got a right special way of talking, don't she?'

'I reckon she's one o' them highfalutin sorts, pard.'

Cowlick guffawed. 'Could be just a put-on, Marco. She's playing at being educated to tease and tempt us.'

'There's something the world sure don't need . . . an educated woman.'

Constance made a second effort to go around the two men, but they were not dissuaded. They moved to block her from going down the street, and when she pivoted about, Cowlick hurried and prevented her from retreating in that direction too.

'What do you men want?' Constance asked brusquely. 'I'll report you to the sheriff if you don't leave me alone.'

Marco snickered. 'She'll report us to the sheriff, Cowlick.'

His partner laughed. 'Oh, dear me!' he scoffed in a high-pitched voice, 'Please don't tattle to the law. We're plumb afraid of Sheriff Milburn.'

'Skeered to death,' Marco agreed.

Constance was frightened now. These men did not respect the law. They dared to accost a decent woman on the main street of town in full daylight. What would she do if they decided to manhandle her? She had no experience at fending off such men. If they dragged her away, who would come to her rescue?'

CHAPTER SIX

The two bullies moved in, their leering faces close enough that their breath and pungent body odor caused Constance to experience nausea. Desperate, close to hysterical panic, she attempted to summon forth a scream for help, but the cry lodged feebly in her throat.

'Step away, boys,' a cool, yet familiar voice commanded. 'You don't want to be showing a lack of respect for a lady.'

Marco and Cowlick turned their attention to Latimer, who had approached from the alleyway. He displayed an easy smile and added: 'Besides which, the gal is my boss.'

Both men whirled about to confront Latimer, dismissing Constance altogether. Clearly, these two had intended to make trouble and were not surprised in the least that Latimer had come to Constance's aid.

'I'd wager you're joshing us,' Marco taunted

menacingly. 'You think if you stick up for this spunky little filly, she'll reward you with her favors.'

'Marco's right,' Cowlick joined in. 'You're trying to cut in line, buster. We take exception to a gent who don't wait his turn.'

Latimer remained passive, but he also displayed a knowing look. 'All right, boys.' His delivery remained polite. 'It's plain you started bothering the lady because you wanted to start a fight with me.' He sighed, as if resigned to giving them what they wanted. 'Which of you morons is going to throw the first punch?'

Cowlick didn't hesitate; he took a mighty swing with a balled right fist.

Latimer adroitly dodged the wild roundhouse punch. Then latching hold of the man's wrist with one hand, he grabbed Cowlick's shoulder with the other, yanked him forward and gave him a shove. The action of the hard, missed swing already had Cowlick off balance. Latimer's action propelled him right into Marco. The collision was enough to block Marco's attack and Latimer quickly drew his gun.

Using the weapon as a club, Latimer walloped Cowlick on the back of his skull hard enough that he dropped to his knees at Marco's feet. Having a body in his path, Marco jumped awkwardly to get around Cowlick. Latimer matched his reaction with a quick move of his own. He lunged forward and drove his left fist into Marco's jaw. The punch only dazed the brute, but it kept him off balance long enough for Latimer to use the pistol a second time and clout Marco smartly on the side of his head. The man groaned from the blow and sank to the ground next to his friend.

Holstering his gun, Latimer spoke to a rather shocked Constance. 'If you would like to go back to the hotel I'll meet you there in a few minutes.' He shrugged his shoulders. 'Although the sheriff is likely the one who decided to sic these two dogs on us, he'll have to go through the motions of reprimanding them for their bad manners.'

'Uh,' Constance murmured, still shaken and discomposed by the encounter, 'whatever you say, Mr Latimer.'

'And, Miss Dewitt,' Latimer's words caused her to pause, 'may I say you look exceptionally nice.'

Constance swallowed to keep her thundering heart in her chest and glanced nervously at the two men who were moaning and half-conscious on the dusty street. Finding her voice, she managed, 'T-thank you, Mr Latimer.'

Once the lady had hurried off towards the hotel Latimer removed the gunbelts and weapons from the two rowdies and got them on their feet. Although groggy from being pistol whipped, the pair were able to stagger to the jail.

Hap was watching the office when the trio arrived. He appeared to find the whole situation amusing, but did his job and herded the two men into the second jail cell.

'Most prisoners we've had at one time in a coon's age,' he remarked to Latimer.

'Tell Milburn they insulted a lady and attacked me on the street,' Latimer explained to Hap, placing the prisoner's gunbelts on the desk. 'Fortunately, no one was seriously hurt.'

'Tell that to my aching head,' Marco whined.

'Me too,' Cowlick joined in. 'Damn! Now I know what an egg feels like just before the yoke hits the skillet.'

'Sorry, fellas,' Latimer called back. 'You should have left well enough alone when I asked you to stop pestering the lady.'

'We'd have stomped a hole in your gullet if you'd have fought us fair,' Marco complained.

'The way I was taught, two against one isn't considered a fair fight,' Latimer retorted.

Hap chuckled at the exchange. 'I'll tell the sheriff what happened, Latimer. Reckon it'll cost them boys ten dollars each to get out of jail.'

'Twenty good reasons not to molest an innocent lady,' Latimer suggested.

'That's a good one,' Hap said gleefully. 'Yep, that's a dandy.'

Latimer left the jail, but he was concerned about what the sheriff and his men might try next. If they dared to haze a respectable lady in full view of the entire town, what was there to stop one of them from shooting him from ambush and claiming self-defence?

Lat, old buddy, he thought to himself, *You'd best play this hand real close to the vest. One slip and it could mean the end for you and both of the Dewitts.*

Janus scowled at Milburn, while Cowlick and Marco, having been released, were heading off to Pine's Palace to drink some medicine for their aching heads. As soon as he and the sheriff were alone, he vented his frustration over their actions.

'Of all the stupid stunts,' he wailed. 'What were you thinking, having those two blundering idiots accost a woman right on the street?'

'They were only trying to bait Latimer into coming to her defence. The idea was for them to break a few of his bones and beat him half to death.'

'Yes, and the plan certainly worked to perfection, didn't it?'

'Look, Judge, I knew Latimer was a good shot, but who could have known he would take down a couple hardcases like Marco and Cowlick without breaking a sweat? Neither of them even hit him . . . not once!'

'You do know there are a few people around town who don't approve of how we run things. A stunt like this only makes it worse.'

Milburn dismissed the judge's concern. 'There's nobody of any importance to oppose us.'

'There's Brinkerhoff and Farnsworth!'

The sheriff grunted his contempt. 'Brinkerhoff only has one employee – Sam Gundy, the stage driver. As for Farnsworth, he's a retired army surgeon and the town mortician. They are hardly the kind of men who will raise an army against us.'

'Brinkerhoff sent the telegram to the Dewitt family,' Janus reminded him. 'And I saw Latimer going over to speak to Farnsworth. You underestimated the man once. We can't take him or some of our more moral citizens too lightly.'

'The trial tomorrow makes everything completely legal, Judge. It's to our advantage to have Sheldon's sister here.' He outlined his viewpoint. 'Don't you see? With her attending the trial, there won't be anyone left to protest when we hang Sheldon for murder.'

'I hope you're right.'

Milburn displayed an arrogant expression. 'I spoke to Francis about Latimer's visit. He said he stuck to the story about witnessing the shooting. There's no way the man can defend Dewitt. The noose is as good as around the prisoner's neck. Once you pronounce him guilty, all of our troubles will be over and done with.'

Janus wiped his moist brow. It seemed he had been sweating ever since Latimer and the Dewitt woman showed up. He'd be glad to put this behind him so he could relax and appreciate what they had accomplished.

The eve of the trial was especially hard for
Constance. She had taken a meal over to Sheldon
and spent some time visiting with him. Then she
returned to her room. After pacing and fretting for a
long while she went down the hall to Latimer's room.
Taking a deep breath, she boldly tapped on his door.

There wasn't a sound from the other side. Then,
just as she was thinking that he must be asleep or not
in his room, the door suddenly flew open. Latimer
stood poised, his gun ready for use. Seeing her in the
hallway, he lowered it at once.

'Did you never hear of asking *Who is it?* Mr
Latimer?'

He displayed a sheepish expression. 'Someone
could have had a gun to your head and forced you to
answer.'

'I would have warned you if that had been the
case,' she assured him.

'And how would you have done that?' he wondered aloud.

She had a ready answer. 'I'd have called you by
your first name.'

Latimer moved back to allow her to enter. After
looking quickly to make sure no one was watching,
Constance stepped inside the cubicle and he closed
the door behind her. She inspected the room and
was impressed at seeing that his suit jacket had been

brushed clean and was hanging on a clothing hook.

There was both a pan and a pitcher of water sitting on the room's washing stand, but Latimer had not yet gotten ready for bed. He replaced his gun in the holster, hanging next to the head of the neatly made bed, pivoted about and waited for her to state the purpose of her visit.

Constance discovered she was still holding her breath and released the air, beginning to breathe normally.

'I hope you'll forgive the intrusion, but, with Shelly's trial in the morning, I can't imagine being able to sleep.'

Latimer glanced about awkwardly, not inviting her to sit down. How could he when the only possible place to sit was on the bed? He offered not a word, waiting for her to continue.

'I had three brothers and an older sister,' Constance began. 'But Shelly is the only one I ever spent time with, growing up. We came along late in our parents' lives, a year apart, while our siblings were ten to sixteen years older than us. Mom married Dad at fifteen,' she explained, to clarify the wide range of ages in the children.

'Both of my older brothers went off to the war and died in the battle at Gettysburg. Our sister married and moved to California when we were not yet in our teens. Dad wanted Shelly to work at the bank, but he was never much good at adding sums or sitting behind a desk. I ended up doing most of the work at the bank, while Shelly ran around trying to earn a living at all manner of occupations.

'He became a faro dealer and then a salesman for farm equipment. Next he tried his hand at raising prize bulls and even worked on a riverboat for a time. None of his ventures paid off and his purpose in being here was a frivolous hunting trip to bag a trophy elk or bear – prize antlers or a hide he could hang on a wall back home.'

'He was the drifter while you were the solid home-body,' Latimer summarized. 'I can't imagine that you worked all the time. What about courting?' he asked bluntly. 'I reckon men in St Louis line up like fence posts just for a dance or to spend some time with you.'

Constance lowered her eyes, suddenly uncertain, lacking her usual confidence when talking to a man. It struck her as odd that she should react so strongly to Latimer's mere mention of courting. Why was that?

'I've had a good many suitors,' she admitted. 'Some were quite charming and sincere, but . . .' the hint of a smile played on her lips, 'you're the first man I've ever been alone with in a hotel or boarding room.'

'We're even on that count,' Latimer allowed. 'I've never had a lady in my room before either.' He grinned at his comment. 'Well, actually, I did have a woman stay with me one time. She and her two kids shared my room back when I was working at a way station. We had a hard blizzard and near a dozen folks were stuck with us for three days.' He added, to clarify, 'I ended up sleeping on the floor.'

Constance found his admission a genuinely touching story. 'That's what you did before riding shotgun for a living? You ran a rest stop for an express company?'

Latimer told her how Ramble had collected him after the steamboat accident.

'How dreadful to have lost your entire family at only ten years of age,' she sympathized.

'Two hundred people died that day. The steamboat captain's body was blown six hundred feet by the explosion. I was lucky Ramble found me and took me on like his own son.'

'Is he the one who taught you how to shoot and defend yourself?'

Latimer enlightened her about how he had become so proficient both with his fists and with guns.

Constance was appalled. 'Forced to fight other boys, and then full grown men while still in your teens? It's . . . it seems a terrible way to raise a child.'

'Ramble wanted me to be able to take care of myself,' he excused his adoptive father's actions.

'And your ability to defend my brother? How much do you know about being a lawyer?'

'The winters were long and cold at the way station and I did a lot of reading to pass the time. I've studied a number of cases and even managed to sit in at a trial or two when I was traveling with the stage. Also, I've talked to a few jack-leg lawyers, as well as a couple high society attorney types over the years. I know enough about the law to get the job done tomorrow.'

Constance bore into him with her dark chocolate eyes ablaze, as if she was trying to see right into his soul. 'Do you really think you can save my brother from a noose?' she asked in a mere whisper.

Latimer wondered how it would be to see the same yearning in the lady's eyes that he felt, the kind that stirred his being to the core. She was the most desirable woman he had ever met, and although she was much too good for him, he would have done anything in the world to make her happy.

'Mr Latimer?' she queried, 'Did you hear me?'

He swallowed his craving and mentally scolded himself for daydreaming. 'Uh, yeah, I did.'

'Well?'

Mustering up the best supportive look he could, he answered, 'I've a plan to clear Sheldon's name, Miss Dewitt. I can't promise you that this won't turn ugly and maybe come to a fight, but I won't let them hang your brother.'

'How can you promise that?'

'Because he's innocent,' Latimer said simply.

71

Constance leaned forward so quickly that Latimer had no chance to prepare himself. When her lips touched his cheek, it felt as if a dozen doves took flight from inside his chest. The lady pulled back at once and smiled, her eyes brimming with tears.

'I . . . I can never thank you enough, Mr Latimer.'

'Yes, ma'am,' he managed in reply.

Then she whirled about and went out of the room. It left Latimer alone and feeling better than he could ever remember.

CHAPTER SEVEN

The trial was held at Pine's Palace saloon at nine the next morning. The tables had been put aside and the room was furnished mostly with chairs and a few benches. Judge Poe sat behind a desk, with a chair placed for those giving testimony to his left. The jury was in a group to his right and included both Cowlick and Marco. It was apparent that the hearing was to be over and done with in short order, with Sheldon likely being sentenced to hang the following day. It reaffirmed Latimer's determination to proceed with his plan.

Constance sat next to the Brinkerhoff family, who were about the only people they had met who didn't seem to think Sheldon was guilty. Latimer had the chair next to Sheldon, but didn't speak to him while the court called the witnesses against his client.

First off, the sheriff explained how he and Hap had been called to the murder site. Amble Graham

73

was dead and the gun was lying next to his body. After speaking to the only witness, Francis Bellows, they had arrested Sheldon in his room.

Latimer asked two questions of the sheriff. 'Did you learn of any reason why my client should want to kill Mr Graham?'

'No.'

'And you say Mr Dewitt was in bed asleep when you arrested him?'

'Couldn't say if he was asleep or not,' Milburn replied. 'We got the spare key from the clerk and went in with guns drawn. Dewitt was in bed when we entered the room.'

'Thank you, Sheriff Milburn. I've no more questions for you.'

Next was the banker, Francis. He told how he had been walking past the alleyway, heard an argument and saw the shooting take place. He stated positively that the man who had killed Graham was the accused, Sheldon Dewitt.

'That is all the testimony needed for the prosecution,' Janus declared. 'Do you have any questions for the witness, Mr Latimer?'

'Yes,' Latimer said, rising to his feet. He addressed the banker. 'I wonder how you saw the shooting so clearly? It was well after dark.'

'The window from Pine's Palace faces the front of the street,' Francis replied. 'It lit up the alleyway so I was able to see as plain as day.'

Latimer approached the witness chair and stopped a couple steps away. 'Would you mind telling the court exactly what you saw.'

'It's like I said, Dewitt pulled a gun and shot Graham at near point-blank range,' Francis maintained.

Latimer had Sheldon stand up and he walked over next to him. 'Direct me so that I am in the exact same position for the shooting,' Latimer prompted the man. Then he stood one step away from Sheldon on his left side and extended his right hand, with his index finger acting as if it was the gun. 'Is this about right?'

Francis stared at him, as if trying to decide what this was all about. 'Uh, yeah, maybe a few inches closer.'

Latimer made the adjustment and enquired, 'Now, did you see if he pulled the gun from his coat pocket or waistband?'

'I didn't actually see him draw the weapon,' Francis admitted. 'The two were arguing and it caught my attention. By the time I spotted the two of them, Mr Dewitt had his gun pointed at Amble Graham.'

Latimer continued to stand with his right hand pointed at Sheldon. 'Just like this?' he asked. When Francis said yes, he asked, 'Did Mr Dewitt have anything in his other hand?'

'No. He just pointed the gun and fired.'

'Think carefully, Mr Bellows,' Latimer warned the man. 'Am I posed in precisely the same position as my client was when he shot Mr Graham?'

'Yes,' Francis agreed impatiently, 'that's how it was exactly.'

'Thank you, Mr Bellows,' Latimer said. 'I have no more questions for you.'

Janus waved to Francis that he was finished and both the banker and Sheldon returned to their seats. Latimer waited for them to take their chairs, then turned to the judge.

'Your honor, I would like your permission to perform two quick tests. It is the only defence I have to offer.'

The judge frowned. 'You don't have any witnesses?'

'If you'll allow me the two demonstrations, no witnesses will be required. As I said, it's the entire defence on Mr Dewitt's behalf.'

The judge flicked a glance at Milburn, who offered a slight shrug of indifference. As far as he was concerned the trial was all but over.

'Make it quick, Mr Latimer. I won't tolerate any deliberate acts of deception.'

Latimer, having prepared for the test ahead of time, had a large white table napkin ready. He draped the cloth over a thick piece of wood he had previously placed against one wall of the courtroom. He then retrieved the murder weapon, which had been submitted to the judge as part of the evidence against Sheldon. As Janus displayed a perplexed expression, he loaded one of the four bullets that was lying next to the revolver. Before anyone could object he walked over, stood approximately three feet from the cloth, and pulled the trigger.

The explosion was extremely loud inside the room. Without pausing, Latimer returned the weapon to the judge's desk. Janus opened his mouth to question him, but Latimer held up a hand to stop him.

'Sorry about the noise,' he told Janus. 'I won't be shooting off a gun a second time.'

The judge glowered at him. 'Let's not drag this out. Proceed with your second demonstration.'

Instead of offering a word of explanation, Latimer removed a small rock from his pocket and handed it to Sheldon.

'Would you throw this stone against the wall. Try not to hit a window, just throw it hard.'

Sheldon looked even more baffled than the judge. He gave the rock a toss and the rock bounced off of the wall.

'No!' Latimer scolded his lame effort and handed him a second stone. 'Throw it as hard as you can.'

Sheldon rose up to his feet and launched the rock hard enough that it hit with a bang. When he sat back down Latimer turned to the judge.

'That concludes my demonstrations, Judge.'

Janus displayed complete puzzlement. 'So how does shooting a piece of white cloth or having Mr Dewitt throw rocks add up to a defence?'

'Thank you for asking, Your Honor,' Latimer replied. 'I'd be happy to explain.'

Janus sighed resignedly and said, 'Do so quickly and be done with it.'

Latimer addressed the crowd, rather than the judge. 'No one has come forward with any reason as to why my client would have killed Mr Graham. In fact, Mr Dewitt told me the only conversation between himself and Mr Graham was concerning how much it would cost to rent a couple of horses for a hunting trip.' Latimer shook his head with disbelief. 'Then, my client doesn't run and hide after the shooting but leaves the murder weapon behind and calmly goes to bed. Not exactly the actions of a man who had just murdered someone.'

'Ahem,' Judge Poe interrupted. 'We are concerned with facts here, Mr Latimer, not your unfounded speculation upon the events.'

Latimer nodded his head in agreement, walked to the white cloth and held it up for those in the makeshift courtroom to see. Turning slowly around the room, he instructed, 'Everyone take a good look at this cloth. There are scorch marks and bits of powder embedded in a wide circle about the bullet hole from the murder weapon.' Once he had shown the cloth to the jury, he placed it next to the gun on

78

the judge's desk, then picked up a plain cotton shirt.

'Doctor Farnsworth provided me with this. It's the shirt Mr Graham was wearing at the time he was shot,' Latimer explained to the court. 'It was a warm evening and he was not wearing a jacket or vest, just this shirt.' He then again showed it to everyone in the room. 'There are no powder residue or burn marks on Mr Graham's shirt, only a clean bullet hole and a bit of dried blood.' He emphasized, 'This is completely different from the cloth I fired at with the very same gun.' He allowed a moment of silence so everyone could understand the meaning. Then he concluded, 'Which means the shooter was not standing anywhere close to Graham when the fatal bullet was fired.'

Janus began to bluster again, but Latimer cut him off by raising his voice. 'And finally,' he maintained the floor, 'Everyone in this room witnessed Sheldon Dewitt throw two stones . . . with his *left* hand. Francis Bellows clearly indicated that the gun was in the killer's right hand. Standing right here, pretending to aim a gun at the defendant, I asked him if more than once if I was in the correct position. He said I was, meaning the man he thought did the shooting was right-handed.'

Turning to face the people in the courtroom, Latimer held up his right hand with three fingers. 'There's no motive for the killing.' He lowered the first finger. 'No powder or scorching about the wound.' He lowered the second finger. 'And the man Francis saw shoot Mr Graham was right-handed, standing less than three feet away.' He looked over his shoulder at the judge and finished, 'The only possible conclusion is that the shooter was someone other than my client, Sheldon Dewitt.'

To allow the possibility that the banker hadn't lied outright, Latimer gave him a courtesy exit. 'I would suggest that someone else fired the shot from further down the darkened alleyway, then they threw the gun where it would land near the body. Francis Bellows must have seen the muzzle flash and assumed the shot came from the man he thought was Sheldon Dewitt.'

'That's ridic—' Janus began, but stopped from finishing an indignant outburst. He closed his mouth, acutely aware of several shouts and the hostile muttering of the crowd. One look at the jury told him they would never find Dewitt guilty, even though several were sitting as jurors to do just that. After a short pause he cleared his throat and tapped his gavel to quiet the spectators.

'It is apparent to the court,' he proclaimed through clenched teeth, 'that we have the wrong man in custody. The case against Mr Dewitt is hereby dismissed!'

Sheldon jumped up, grabbed Latimer's hand and pumped it up and down. Constance arrived and hugged her brother in elated celebration. Latimer began to step away so they could have the moment alone, but the young woman whirled about and threw her arms around his neck. Caught unawares by her jubilance, he was unable to react when she kissed him full on the mouth.

She pulled back at once, smiling brightly. 'You did it!' she cried. 'You really did it!'

Latimer suffered a whirlwind of emotions, and was momentarily numb. He ducked his head blushingly and muttered, 'Well, we both knew he was innocent.'

'I'm buying lunch for you both,' she asserted happily. 'Let's get out of this place.'

Milburn and Janus stood together after the courtroom had cleared. They were joined by Cowlick and Marco, both grumbling about the outcome of the trial. Francis also lingered behind and added his own complaint.

'That went about as bad as it could!' he said.

Janus growled angrily, 'It's not my fault. I couldn't very well convict a man with the evidence Latimer presented.'

'Who'd have figured him for the smarts to pull off something like this?' Marco put in. 'No way we could have gotten a guilty plea from the other jury members.'

'Latimer knows I lied,' Francis lamented loudly. 'That man is going to think I had a hand in Graham's murder.'

'He doesn't know anything,' Milburn argued. 'He got what he wanted: he cleared the woman's brother of the murder charge. The three of them will probably leave town on tomorrow's stage.'

'I don't like it,' Janus fumed. 'Everyone in town now knows we tried to frame an innocent man. That isn't going to sit well with a good many people around here. Amble Graham was pretty much a hermit, but he had a few friends. They are going to want to know who really did the killing.'

Milburn did some quick thinking. 'We'll find someone to take the blame . . . another drifter, or we might even round up a renegade Indian. We'll concoct the very story Latimer used.' He turned his attention to Francis. 'You saw Sheldon Dewitt point at Graham and thought he actually had a gun in his hand. Remember, you said you didn't see him draw the weapon.'

Francis nodded his understanding. 'All right, I see what you're saying. The flash from the muzzle was further down the alley. It looked like Dewitt had fired, but it came from the darkness.'

'So much for us being held accountable,' Milburn commented. 'We'll still look like we were only doing our jobs.'

'What if Latimer sticks around?' Cowlick asked. 'That man has shown he's quick with his wits, as well as with his fists and gun.'

'Why should he stay here?' Janus wanted to know.

'He got what he wanted. He saved the woman's brother from a noose.'

'I was only asking,' Cowlick said.

'Don't sweat something that hasn't come to pass,' Milburn told him. 'However, you and Marco had better keep an eye on those three. . . just in case they do decide to stick around.' He paused, then changed his mind. 'Wait. We better bring in Santeen and Rivers to keep watch. Latimer won't know them by sight.'

'They are out at Graham's place, with the two hired hands, rounding up Graham's livestock,' Marco reported. 'I'll ride out and get them back here pronto.'

'Good thinking, Sheriff,' Cowlick agreed. 'Rivers and Santeen can watch those three until the stage leaves tomorrow.'

'Get going,' Milburn ordered.

No sooner were they out of the room than Francis again showed his pusillanimity. 'I'm going to need some protection. There are some who will think I conspired in Graham's murder because I lied about seeing Dewitt do the killing.'

'We covered that,' Janus reminded him. 'You only thought you saw the man fire a gun.'

'I doubt anyone will actually believe that story, not with Latimer making me look the fool. There will be questions, and I want someone near by to keep me from being badgered or threatened.'

Milburn stifled his impatience with the weasel-like man. 'I'll have Hap hang around the bank. When you leave, he can tag along to your house and make sure no one gives you any trouble.'

Francis bobbed his head nervously. 'That ought to do it. No one is going to mess with Hap.'

'Fine.' Janus ended the meeting. 'We'll bide our time until the Dewitts and Latimer leave town. Then we'll find another sucker to take the blame for killing Graham.'

All being in agreement, the men left the court-room.

CHAPTER EIGHT

Constance noticed Latimer was not much for conversation. As she and Sheldon discussed going back home, the taciturn Latimer offered not a word. She knew part of the reason . . . the kiss she had planted on his lips. It had been impulsive, reckless and abandoned, but the joy of having Latimer clear her brother of murder had overwhelmed her common sense and usual sense of propriety.

'You've been very silent during our celebration, Mr Latimer,' she said, trying to relieve some of the pent-up tension between them. 'You did a wonderful job, dismantling the case against Shelly.'

'I'll say!' Sheldon seconded her comment. 'How did you know I was left-handed?'

'Ramble's callus was on his right thumb from playing the guitar, yours was on your left.'

'Yeah, right!' Sheldon laughed, still somewhat giddy an hour after being found innocent. 'I never thought of that.'

Constance complimented him on his performance. 'You certainly made the banker look bad, even though you offered him a plausible vindication for his testimony. The man was undoubtedly lying to help convict an innocent man.'

'We were lucky there are some honest people in Baxterville,' Latimer said. 'Brinkerhoff sent the telegram that saved your life, and the doctor gave me the shirt Graham was wearing, knowing I would use it to beat the murder charge. Both men told me there are others here who want honest law and order.'

'So tell me, Latimer,' Sheldon said. 'Do you have any idea as to why Graham was killed?'

'According to Brinkerhoff there's a rumor that the railroad intends to run a spur up into Montana and the Dakotas. With a lot of mining going on up that way and some big herds of cattle to be shipped, the spur could be quite profitable.'

'What's that got to do with Graham?'

'He owned the land between the two ranges of mountains, the only valley to the north for a hundred miles around. It's the perfect route for the railroad to use when they lay their tracks.'

Sheldon understood. 'And that makes the land worth a fortune.'

'Either he wouldn't sell or the men involved in his death weren't of a mind to pay for his place. Now the bank has the deed to his property.'

'Yes,' Constance interjected, 'what a coincidence that the beneficiary of Graham's death just happens to be the same man who identified Shelly as the man's murderer.'

'I think Bellows might talk,' Latimer said. Adding, 'With a little encouragement.'

'You think he killed Graham?' Sheldon asked.

'No, he doesn't strike me as a man capable of killing. However, he likely knows who did the shooting.'

'I'm sure he'll be protected,' Constance remarked. 'The judge and sheriff will likely let the matter of Graham's death pass without further interest.'

'Probably,' Latimer replied.

'You're a very brave and astute man,' Sheldon told him. 'I have never met another man who would dare take on such odds to prove a stranger's innocence.'

'Not only brave, but bordering on foolhardy!' Constance professed, her voice revealing a trace of ire. 'A man with less fighting skill would have gotten himself killed.'

Latimer retorted, 'There has to be the rule of law and it has to be the same for everyone. When you put on a badge you take an oath to uphold what is right. The law isn't something to be used by underhanded crooks or those with money and power, it's the measure of a society itself.'

Constance was taken back at his poetic delivery. 'Mr Latimer,' she said quietly, 'I do believe there is more to you than meets the eye.'

'Ramble used to make up sayings like that,' Latimer admitted. 'He believed in the goodness of man. With a grin, 'But he ensured that I could fight and shoot, because of the evil of man too.'

Sheldon and Constance both laughed. Their mirth caused Latimer to relax and smile back. He'd never been around a woman like her before. Something told him, he would never be around another like her either.

Sam Gundy arrived late that day with the stage. Latimer was there to meet him. Once the team was put away he and Hans Brinkerhoff spent a few minutes talking with Sam out by the barn. Latimer asked them what they knew about the men who ran the town.

Sam eyed Latimer curiously. 'You ain't taking a hand in this game?' He whistled under his breath. 'Man, that would be like spitting in the devil's soup bowl. You'll end up with your name on a wooden cross a half-mile south of here – the town's cemetery.'

'You've been making this run for the last two years, Sam,' said Latimer. 'And,' turning to Brinkerhoff, 'running this express office, you have to know what's going on.'

'I know you caused a lot of trouble by getting the

Dewitt boy off from a murder charge,' Brinkerhoff replied. 'I know that you're being watched right now by one of Milburn's hired guns. I know that if Sam or I was to open our mouths, we'd likely end up buried next to you on boot hill.'

'How many men are we talking about – four . . . five . . . a dozen or more?'

Brinkerhoff looked at Sam, but his driver allowed him to answer. 'Three men control the town – the judge, the sheriff and the banker. But there is a deputy and five or six others who are always handy when needed. You've met Cowlick and Marco,' he pointed out. 'The guys watching things right now are Rivers and Santeen. But,' he emphasized, 'the three Doolans have been in town since before Graham was killed. They are a bad lot and, when added to the others, it makes a heap of firepower to tackle all by your lonesome.'

Latimer asked, 'What about Bo Janks? He was one of the men who tried to abduct Miss Dewitt from the stage. Who does he work for?'

'Bo is . . . was,' Brinkerhoff corrected quickly, 'related to Janus Poe. Doc Farnsworth once told me that Bo mentioned being his cousin or nephew. Whenever he was in town, Milburn would put him to work as a favor to the judge.'

Latimer smiled at the news. 'So there is a link.'

'You find enough links,' Sam warned, 'and you'll have a chain long enough to hang yourself.'

'Thanks, fellows. I appreciate the information.'

Sam snorted. 'What information? I didn't say a word, 'cause I ain't gonna help you to commit suicide.'

Brinkerhoff nodded in the direction of the express office. 'I've got a customer waiting,' he said and left the two of them.

Latimer waited until Brinkerhoff was inside the office before he turned to Sam. 'Could you do me one favor?'

'You mean one that won't get me kilt?'

'I'm going to board the stage tomorrow morning so it will look like I'm leaving with the Dewitts. Then, once we get about a mile out of town, you can drop me off. With a little luck, I'll be able to get back here and avoid detection until I can speak to the banker alone.'

Sam showed a grim reluctance but gave a positive bob of his head. 'I can always say you jumped out of the coach when I wasn't looking, so I didn't have no idea where you went.'

'Thanks, Sam. I owe you.'

'Yeah, I'm a peach I am . . . helping you to get in a fix where you are sure enough going to wind up explaining to St Peter as to how come you got to heaven thirty years ahead of schedule.'

For the second night in a row, about the time Latimer was getting ready for bed, there came a knock at the door.

'Yeah?' he asked, sticking close to where he had hung his gunbelt and Remington over the bedpost.

'May I speak with you, Mr Latimer?' came Constance's voice from the hallway.

Latimer still had on his lawyer clothes, except that he had removed the jacket. He opened the door to discover that Constance had changed her outfit and was now attired in a relatively austere yellow dress. The gown was about the only thing that was plain about the woman. Her raven-colored hair had been brushed to a healthy sheen and a hint of rouge pinkened her sinuous lips. Behind her black lashes her enticing dark eyes were twin pools of liquid light, brilliant, yet seductively serene. When she flashed a timid smile in greeting, it devastated Latimer's usually calm demeanor.

'Miss Dewitt.' He managed the greeting and tried not to stumble over his words. 'I didn't expect to see you until we boarded the stage.'

'I thought we should settle accounts in private. May I come in?'

He hastily backed up and held the door. As soon as she was inside the room, he took a deep breath and closed the door. Here he was again, in the presence of a woman who could send his soul skyward to the heavens with a single word, gesture or glance.

Constance opened her handbag and removed some bills and a piece of paper. She handed them to

Latimer and explained, 'One hundred dollars for the week and a bank note for five hundred more. You can deposit the note or cash it at most banks, or any Wells Fargo office.'

'Ma'am, that's way too much money for what little I did.'

'*What little you did*!' she objected. 'You saved me from three would-be kidnappers, men who would most certainly have murdered me after they received their ransom. You also stopped two bullies from molesting me in the street!' She moved to within arm's distance and gazed directly into his eyes. 'And you saved my brother from being framed and hanged for a murder he didn't commit. How can you stand there and tell me I'm paying you too much?'

Latimer was surprised by her outburst, but Ramble had told him never to back water, whether it be Indians, bandits or a tougher man. Now, he had never mentioned the fair sex, but Latimer figured Ramble would have insisted he hold his ground against one of them too . . . even one as desirable and beautiful as Constance Dewitt.

'You didn't take into account the personal rewards I received by taking this journey with you, miss,' he responded to her argument. 'You have treated me like your escort, rather than a hired hand. You have shared your company and even kissed me.' Latimer shook his head. 'Any unhitched man who didn't figure a kiss from you was worth getting killed for don't rightly deserve the title of being called a man.'

Constance frowned uncertainly and backed up a step. 'The kiss?' she murmured, unable to hide an immediate flush. 'I-I had forgotten all about it.'

Latimer chuckled. 'You need to practise lying a whole lot more if you ever expect to ever be any good at it.'

The crimson hue washed slightly higher up her cheeks and she lowered her eyes. 'Of course I remember kissing you. But I explained, it was impetuous and lacked forethought.'

'It don't make it any easier for me, Miss Dewitt. Being kissed by you was the high point of my life. The fact that it meant nothing to you doesn't help me to forget about it.'

Those words caused her head to snap up. 'What do you mean – *meant nothing to me?*' Her face transformed into a hard mask. 'I would never kiss a man as payment or as some kind of game. I believe a kiss is sacred, either saved for passion or,' she visibly sought the right word, '. . . or deep appreciation,' she finished.

'All right,' Latimer allowed. 'I'll try telling myself the kiss was gratitude and let it go at that.'

His response didn't appear to suit the woman. Latimer wondered what kind of measuring stick the female of the species used when it came to interacting with a man. It sure wasn't the same as Ramble had taught.

'I owe you an apology for the intimate display and my rash behavior, because you have not made a single . . .' she once more searched for the right term, 'romantic overture towards me,' she concluded.

It was Latimer's turn to frown. 'You wanted me to sing an opera type tune?'

Constance threw her hands in the air. 'I give up!' she cried. 'I should have plainly stated that I made a complete fool of myself by kissing you and been done with this. Good night, Mr Latimer.'

But Latimer was between her and the door. With this being a war of words, he knew he wasn't properly armed for battle. His only option was to make it physical and see if that got him a black eye or something else to balance the scales.

He grabbed the woman by her shoulders and drew her close to his chest. 'I sing like a cat with its tail in a bear trap,' he said huskily. 'But I've wanted to do this since I first laid eyes on you.' He slanted his head enough to lean in and kiss Constance full on the mouth. To his utter disbelief and elation, the lady did not resist. Instead, she met his desperate act with utter composure and a firm pressing of her lips against his own.

They stood together for a few long moments, Constance in his arms and Latimer's head in the clouds. When she leaned back from him, he hastily released his hold and moved aside so she could make her exit.

'Good night, Dean,' Constance said softly, with no mention of his brazen behavior. 'I'll see you in the morning.'

Latimer remained dumbstruck, unable to even manage an 'uh-huh'. When once more alone in the room, his heart was still drifting among the stars.

'Lat, old boy,' he whispered aloud, 'you've been missing something better than anything Ramble ever told you about.'

Hap had just dropped off to sleep in the one of the cell bunks when Milburn arrived. The sheriff had watched the stage pull out early that morning, so the episode with the Dewitts and Latimer was finished.

His moving about roused Hap. Hap muttered and grumbled, but came stumbling out of the cell. His eyes were red from having had so little sleep, but he quickly assumed his usual sunny disposition.

'Hey, Sheriff,' he greeted Milburn. 'How is everything this morning?'

'Now that our three troublemakers have left on the stage, it's shaping up to be a fine day, Hap. You have any trouble last night? Anyone come snooping around trying to talk to Bellows?'

'Naw. He did some banking type stuff with the Rileys,' (the couple who worked at his bank), 'then had a meal by himself at the Mexican's tavern. No one came round atall. Once he was in bed, I kept

95

watch until Marco showed up at midnight and he took over from there.'

'I saw Bill Riley taking some mail from the bank to the express office.' Milburn didn't elaborate, as Bill was usually the one to take any mail or money transfers to Brinkerhoff's office. 'Didn't see Latimer or the Dewitts do anything out of the ordinary and they all got on the stage. It looks as if they are all out of our hair.'

'You want me to watch Francis any more today?'

'No need, with Latimer gone. I'll give him some time alone and maybe have Marco keep an eye on his place this evening. I don't expect any trouble.'

'You got any idea who really did shoot Amble Graham, Sheriff?'

Milburn feigned a sincere interest. 'We will keep looking and talking to people. Maybe we'll get lucky.'

'Funny thing, if that Dewitt fellow was standing so close to Graham, how come he didn't see who took the shot?'

'I questioned him about it after we arrested him,' Milburn said. 'He kept saying he had been in bed the whole time. I think Francis must have seen someone in the alley who looked like Dewitt.'

Hap bobbed his head in agreement. 'That Latimer sure played a good hand, proving Dewitt hadn't done the shooting. And he sure enough taught Marco and Cowlick not to pester a lady. The guy is smart and tough. What do you think, Sheriff?'

'I think I'm glad he's gone,' Milburn replied. 'A man like him is dangerous to everyone. Cowlick and Marco are lucky he didn't kill them both, the way he did Bo Janks and those two bounty hunters.'

'You need me to do anything for you today?' Hap asked, dismissing Latimer and Graham's murder. 'My ma wants me to build a new fence. The milk cow got out again yesterday and trampled Mrs Farnsworth's flowers.'

'I'll keep an eye on things, Hap,' Milburn offered. 'You go help your mother with her fence.'

That put a wide smile on the deputy's face. 'OK, I'll sure enough get it done before sundown, in case you need me for something tonight.'

The sheriff watched the dull-witted man hurry from the office. Hap could be tough when called upon, but his biggest asset was that he trusted Milburn completely. Until Latimer proved Dewitt's innocence, Hap had ignored every word the prisoner said. Better still, he forgot much of what he heard. A more alert deputy would have wondered about Sheldon murdering a man and then calmly going to bed.

Stoking up the fire in the pot-bellied stove, Milburn poured some water in the coffee pot. Even though Dewitt had been found innocent, Graham was dead and they had gained control of his ranch. One day soon he, Francis and Janus would be rich men. The notion of how he would spend his share of that money danced in his head and brought a smile to his face. Everything was still going as planned.

CHAPTER NINE

Hans Brinkerhoff was about to close for lunch when Latimer slipped inside the express office unseen. The man turned the card in the window to read 'Closed' before he saw Latimer standing back in the shadows of the room.

'Holy Hanna!' he exclaimed. 'I thought you left on the stage?'

'I need a place to hide out until dark. I'm going to talk privately with the banker.'

Brinkerhoff walked away from the single window next to the entrance. With them both out of sight of any passers-by, he displayed a puzzled mien.

'Funny you should mention Bellows. He took his horse from the stable this morning, a short while after the stage pulled out,' the man informed Latimer. 'He sometimes takes a ride out to look over a piece of property, in the event of the owner needing to borrow money . . . that sort of thing.

Unless he tells me otherwise, he pays me to have a kid take the horse out one day a week for exercise.' He cocked his head quickly to one side, indicating he was impressed. 'Finest animal in the country, if you ask me. I believe his mare has some Arabian blood, but a lot more bottom than most. It can run all day and be ready for a race at night.'

'And you say he took the horse this morning?'

'Paid his bill too,' Brinkerhoff said. 'He's always very punctual about that . . . although he is actually a couple days early this month.'

'He didn't say if he was leaving town?'

'Don't know why he would,' Brinkerhoff replied. 'He once told me he lost his only family members to cholera and he's never left the bank for an extended period of time. At least, not since I've been here. The curious thing is, he asked me to keep it quiet.'

Latimer decided to take the man into his confidence. 'I've been deputized by US Marshal Ellington to find out who killed Amble Graham.'

The man grinned. 'I met Konrad once when I was in Rimrock. He seems a good man.' Then he added, 'And he must figure you're a pretty competent man, trusting you to look into a murder case.'

'Yes, but I have to stay out of sight until I know what's going on. If the ones responsible for murdering Graham get spooked, they might start shooting. I'd hate to get some bystanders injured or killed.'

Brinkerhoff understood. 'Sam stays in the shed

100

out back when he doesn't want to pay for a room at the boarding house. I've let a down and out traveler use it on occasion too. You can stay there until nightfall.'

'That would be great.'

'Stick around a few minutes and I'll fix you a plate of food. The wife always makes twice what I can eat for lunch.'

'Much obliged, Hans.'

Brinkerhoff grew serious. 'No, son, it's the least I can do. Graham was a loner, except for a couple of hired hands who helped with his horses. However, he was a decent sort and I'd like to see his killer brought to justice.'

Latimer thanked him a second time and Brinkerhoff headed off to his house, which was next door. As he awaited his return he pondered why Francis Bellows would be needing his horse. Was this something to do with Graham's ranch? If so, why keep it a secret from the sheriff or judge? Something didn't add up, but he would have to wait for dark to find out what was going on.

Sam backed up from the woman and threw up his hands in surrender. 'I didn't know Latimer hadn't told you his plan,' he cried defensively. 'He jumped off when we crossed that first creek, about a mile out of Baxterville.'

Constance did not relent. 'He went back to find

101

out who killed Mr Graham, didn't he.'

Although it was a declaration rather than a question, Sam replied. 'He told me he wanted to slip back and talk to a few people, without the sheriff or judge knowing about it.'

'Because he believes they are responsible for Graham's murder?'

'I don't know nothing about nothing.' Sam continued his plea for mercy. 'He asked me to let him pretend to be heading for Rimrock; that's the only part of his plan I'm aware of.'

'It makes sense he would sneak back,' Sheldon spoke up, trying to calm his sister's agitation. 'He can speak secretly to the banker and anyone else who wants Graham's murderer caught.'

Constance spun on her brother like an enraged cougar. 'He's all alone. If the judge and sheriff are mixed up in this, they have a half-dozen men they can turn loose on Dean.'

Sheldon blinked in surprise. 'Dean?'

Constance swallowed her embarrassment. 'I mean Mr Latimer.'

Sheldon paused while collecting himself and regarded his sister thoughtfully. 'Other than me, I can't remember you calling any man by his first name since we were in school.'

Before she could respond, the express agent came out of the office to speak to Sam. Everyone waited as he approached, holding an envelope in one hand.

'Anyone know where Latimer is at?' the agent asked the three of them. 'Got a letter here with his name on it.'

Constance stepped forward to interrogate the man. 'A letter? From where?'

'It was in the mail sack Sam handed to me,' the man said defensively. 'That means it just arrived from Baxterville.'

Constance did some quick thinking. 'Is Marshal Ellington still in Broken Spoke?'

'Far as I know,' the man answered.

'I need you to send him a telegraph message . . . right now!'

The sun was down but it wasn't full dark when Latimer made a stealthy approach to the banker's house. Making a wide circle to stay out of sight, he unexpectedly came upon the banker's horse in a covert, surrounded by brush and hidden from anyone walking along the main street of town. The animal had been picketed and saddled, complete with rifle, saddlebags and a bedroll. Approaching the fine looking animal, Latimer tested the cinch and discovered it was loose. There was also a bucket of water and a handful of hay near by.

Curious as to what Francis was up to, Latimer crossed the open ground to the back door of his home and pushed his way inside. He was surprised to find the banker was dozing on his couch. At the sound of him entering the room, Francis sat upright, rubbed his eyes, and looked at him in alarm.

'What are you doing here?' he asked.

Latimer would have expected him to be indignant or outraged, but his question was delivered as though out of minor curiosity.

'I had a few questions about Amble Graham's death.'

Francis rose to his feet, went to window and anxiously peered out at the street. 'Did anyone see you come in?'

'Why should anyone be watching?' Latimer wanted to know. 'I pretended to leave town this morning on the stage.'

'It isn't you they are watching,' Francis said, a nervous tremor making his voice quiver. 'I brought my horse over early this morning, but the sheriff has had Marco or Cowlick keeping an eye on me ever since. Soon as it's good and dark, I'm getting out of here.'

'Where are you going?'

'Didn't you read my letter?' the banker queried. 'I explained it all to you.' He turned with his back to the window and lamented, 'I want out. They made me testify in court; they told me to say I had seen the murder. But it was a lie. I never saw anything. I wasn't even outside on the street when the shooting occurred.'

'Who are *they*? Do you mean the judge and sheriff?'

104

The sound of breaking glass was simultaneous with the sound of a gunshot, then came another. Francis doubled over from two bullets striking him in the back. Latimer caught a glimpse of Marco as the man fired several more shots through the window; the bullets were a wild attempt to hit him, but slammed harmlessly into the walls of the room.

Latimer dropped to the floor and did a quick check on the banker. His mouth and eyes were both wide open. He had died instantly.

'There's a killer in the banker's house!' Marco shouted at the top of his lungs. 'He shot Francis and is shooting at me!'

Latimer didn't intend trying to explain an obvious set-up, nor did he think he could survive a fight against the whole town. Another man or two arrived and began shooting. The entire front of the house was bombarded with flying lead.

Latimer crawled madly across the room and out the back door. Then he leapt to his feet and sprinted for the nearest stand of brush. He dove headlong to the ground and scooted behind the heavy under-growth. He lay still, panted for air, and kept watch.

He had been none too quick. Two men suddenly appeared at the back of the house. Even cloaked in the evening shadows, he recognized Marco and the sheriff.

'What the hell, Marco?' Milburn snarled. 'I didn't give the order to kill Francis.'

'I was keeping watch like you told me when I heard voices,' Marco filled in the details. 'Latimer was inside. I heard him and Francis talking. Your banker pal was spilling his guts.'

'What?' Milburn was furious. 'I saw Latimer get on the stage this morning. Are you sure it was him?'

'No doubt about it,' Marco vowed. 'He and Francis were having a talk about Graham's murder. I didn't hear every word that was said, but I managed to shut him up before he could name names.'

Milburn stood with his hands on his hips. 'I'll send Cowlick and a couple men to watch the road to Rimrock. Rivers can take a couple more and watch the valley to the north.'

'We going to get up a posse and try to follow him?' Marco wanted to know.

The sheriff appeared to give the idea some thought. 'We better not involve the good citizens of Baxterville.' His voice was full of menace. 'We don't want him being taken alive. He might start talking and we don't know how much Francis told him.'

Marco contributed, 'The two bronc-busters who worked for Graham are still out at his place. They can tend to the horses and take care of the ranch until this is over.'

'We'll use only our men.'

'You want the Doolan boys to join us?'

Milburn gave an affirmative nod. 'Tracker and Mo used to run down renegades for the army. And they

all three have a special interest in seeing no one dis-
covers Graham's killer. Tell them it's the same deal as
before – a hundred dollars each when Latimer is
dead.'

'You got it, boss,' Marco vowed. 'Soon as we cut
Latimer's trail, we'll have six or more of us on his
tail.'

'I'll tell the townsfolk out front about the special
posse. Francis was not very popular, so I doubt any of
them were going to be eager to volunteer for a
manhunt, especially chasing after a dead shot like
Latimer. I'll break up the crowd and get a couple of
men to take Francis over to Farnsworth for burying.
You go have a talk to the Doolans.' He paused and
asked, 'You did check on Francis to make sure he is
dead?'

Marco displayed a smirk. 'I was only fifteen feet
from the window and put two rounds dead center.
He's done.'

'Latimer must have threatened the craven coward
into telling what he knew,' Milburn said. 'Soon as you
recruit the Doolan boys, start the search. Use
lanterns if you have to, but find us his tracks. I want
you after him at first light.'

Latimer watched Marco hurry off to do as he had
been told while Milburn went through the banker's
house. The sheriff was likely making certain Francis
was dead before he talked to the gathering out front.

Easing back slowly, Latimer remained on his belly

until he reached the edge of the covert. Then he got to his feet and made his way to the waiting horse. Quickly snugging the chinch, he climbed aboard and started the mount around the tangle of brush.

He could still hear some voices from the street near the banker's house and knew there were a number of men surrounding the property. With gunmen watching the trail towards Rimrock and several more blocking his way in the opposite direction, it left him with no choice but the hills north of town. To the east would be riders watching the road to Rimrock. They might spot a rider heading along that route. He was stuck with going north-west and would have to hope he could find a decent trail. With Milburn knowing he had talked to the banker, his men would have orders to kill him on sight.

'Lat,' he muttered to himself, 'this plan of yours didn't work for shucks!'

CHAPTER TEN

It was midmorning by the time Konrad arrived. He and his horse were both jaded and covered with trail dust. Konrad stabled his horse and paid to get a rubdown for the animal. Before he had time to wash up Constance was there to meet him.

'You certainly took your time,' she said abrasively.

'It's sixty miles, lady.' Konrad was indignant. 'I rode all night to get here.'

'Mr Latimer is running for his life,' she informed him. 'We don't have any time to spare.'

Konrad shook the cobwebs from his head. 'Come again? Latimer is on the run?'

'Mr Brinkerhoff sent a message this morning. Someone killed the banker and the crooked law in that town claims it was Mr Latimer. A posse of killers is trying to track him down.' Constance hardened her voice. 'And they won't want to take him alive.'

'Those people seem to be repeating themselves,'

Konrad remarked. 'First your bother is accused of murder and now Latimer.'

'I need for you to open a piece of mail. It might be of vital importance.'

'Mail? For me?'

'No, for Mr Latimer. The banker sent it.'

Konrad shook his head. Maybe he was more tired than he thought. This lady's suggestions made no sense. Instead of arguing – knowing he would only raise her ire and he would lose anyway – he heaved a sigh. 'All right. Who's got the letter?'

Constance almost dragged him to the express office. He then explained to the agent that, as a US Marshal, and considering Latimer was working under cover as his deputy, he had the right to open the letter.

'It might mean his life!' Constance urged, adding encouragement for the agent to comply.

'I reckon it's all right, what with you being his boss and a lawman,' the agent allowed. 'The letter is right here.'

Konrad opened a thick envelope and found two pages. One was a formal-looking document, while the other was Mr Bellows's personal deposition. He read the page and then spoke to Constance.

'The banker admits he lied about seeing your brother shoot Graham. He also claims he was going to leave Baxterville and disappear.' Konrad gritted his teeth. 'Now we know why he was murdered.'

'I knew it!' Constance declared.

Konrad paused to take a closer look at the other sheet of paper. 'Dad blame it! No wonder they are after Latimer. He'll be in for the fight of his life.'

'We have to do something,' Constance said.

'What do you mean . . . we?'

Her expression became fixed. 'I am not going to stand by and let those evil liars and murderers kill Mr Latimer. If it means taking up a weapon myself, I shall do it!'

'The stage doesn't return until tomorrow,' Konrad pointed out.

'I'll rent a horse,' she affirmed, adding with a renewed vigor, 'I'll buy a gun and rent a horse.'

'I know a couple of good men hereabouts.' Konrad tried to sooth her concern. 'I'll deputize them and head for Baxterville, soon as I get something to eat.' He looked around. 'I'll have to get another horse too. Mine won't be up to another forced ride for a few days.'

'I'll go with you.'

'If you insist on going back to Baxterville, you can take the stage. I'm not going to take you along as part of my posse.' She started to open her mouth in protest, but he raised both hands to stop her objection. 'That's the way it's got to be.'

'Fine!' she barked. 'My brother will ride with you.'

'Can he shoot?'

'He is proficient with a rifle; he does a lot of

hunting.' She gave a toss of her head. 'With a handgun, I doubt he could hit anything that was more than ten feet away.'

'I don't know, Miss Dewitt,' Konrad began to argue. This time it was Constance who put up her hands to stop him.

'That's the way it has to be,' she threw his own words back at him. 'It's Shelly or me, Marshal.' She stood defiant and unyielding. 'Take your pick!'

Konrad groaned in defeat and pondered, *Whatever made me think sending Latimer to check out the situation in Baxterville was a good idea?*

The night had been brutal. From sawback sierras to a number of steep palisades, the mountain range was nearly impassable. Latimer spent several hours following animal trails that wound through patches of sage and small groves of buck-brush or pinion. Riding at night had been a slow process, working laboriously to avoid deep coulees or become lost in rugged ravines. He stopped about midnight when he came upon a chaparral with enough grass for his horse and a sheltered spot for tossing down the banker's bedroll.

Up before daylight, Latimer felt the coolness in the air, and the breeze warned of a coming storm. He rummaged through the food Bellows had packed. He ate beans from a can and stuck a couple strips of jerky in his pocket. Once he could make out his surroundings, he set out along the crest of a ridge and turned north. During the hours of darkness he had devised a drastic plan of action. He was in a kill or be killed situation with a passel of hardened gunmen on his trail. No one other than Milburn's goons would be among the posse. That meant he needn't worry about hitting an innocent townsman during any kind of skirmish.

Ramble had once told him that a man forced to defend himself was more dangerous than the ones who went looking for a fight. He once compared it to crossing a bear's path. If you didn't interfere with his direction or purpose, the bear usually ignored you, even to the point of pausing to let you pass. However, back him into a corner or refuse to give way when the bear desired to get past . . . you were instant fodder.

Latimer reached a summit and was able to see a lot of ground below. At last, spotting the kind of terrain for which he had been searching, he turned his horse for the nearest draw. With those in pursuit having to follow his tracks carefully, he would prepare a welcome for the hunters. If they wanted his hide, they were going to have to earn it . . . in blood.

Tracker and Mo took the lead, both men keen on sticking to Latimer's trail. By noon, they had closed the distance to a mile or two. Pausing to rest their mounts, the seven men gathered on a wind-blown plateau that allowed a good view of much of the mountain range.

'Big storm heading our way.' Rivers was the first to speak up. 'I'd say we're going to get wet in the next hour or two.'

'No pattern to his route,' Tracker ignored the forecast and spoke to Marco, who was the man in charge of the chase. 'He wanders aimlessly until he finds an opening through the hills, taking deer trails or following a gorge or coulee here or there. I don't think he has any destination in mind.'

'Probably never been up in this part of the country before,' Marco surmised. 'Maybe he'll turn up a box canyon or end up trapped at the base of a cliff.'

Mo put in an opinion. 'By the looks of it, he's saving his horse in case we get too close. Get out in the open and that part-Arabian of Bellows will leave our nags eating nothing but dust.'

'Bad luck, him somehow ending up with that horse,' Marco said.

Tracker scratched his shaggy head and then ran his hand down to tug lightly at his short beard. He had the wild eyes of a badger, but they were sharp as a hawk's. He took a moment to scan the terrain, then he snorted.

'That coyote has to know we're getting close. He was high enough to catch sight of us on his back trail all morning.'

'Yet he ain't moving any faster,' Mo put in. 'That suggests a thinking man. He is trying to figure a plan.'

Marco laughed without humor. 'What kind of plan can a man come up with when he's got seven men on his tail?'

'I've heard of this Latimer,' Tracker said. 'Prevented six hold-up men from stopping the stage a few months back. The man has some sand in his craw and that means he will fight.'

'He'd be crazy to try and shoot it out with us,' Marco said confidently. 'I think he's looking for a pass or gorge where he can make a run for the nearest fort or maybe one of the towns up in Montana.'

Tracker hadn't gotten his nickname for making mistakes. It was a deadly profession, to follow a desperate man, whether it be an Indian or an outlaw. His first rule of man-hunting was: *don't underestimate your prey.*

'He's headed down to the basin yonder,' he postulated, gauging Latimer's direction. 'No reason to drop so low when it means climbing back up in to the hills again.'

Mo picked up on Tracker's logic. 'He's setting the table for an ambush.'

'It's what I'd do,' Tracker agreed.

'What are you two talking about?' Marco argued. 'If he crosses the open ground we can speed up and cut the distance between him and us in half. We need to catch sight of him before the storm hits.'

Tracker studied the lie of the land for a few long

115

moments before he decided on how to proceed.

'All right, Marco,' he said. 'We'll play the hand two different ways. If you're right, you might get within shooting distance of Latimer when he heads back up the side of the mountain. If he doesn't turn for the high ground, we'll have a chance to circle ahead of him. Either way, we ought to be able to get the man in a crossfire.'

'I'm game.' Marco was eager. 'Soon as we reach the flatland me and the boys will put the spurs to our mounts and make a run at catching Latimer.'

Tracker bobbed his head. 'While you're doing that, the three of us will continue along the crest of the hill to get above him.'

Marco took Cowlick, Rivers and Santeen. The four of them began their descent toward the valley floor.

Jugs Doolan rode up and stopped at his cousin's side. 'Splitting up, huh?'

'Tracker and me smell a trap,' Mo responded.

Jugs grinned at the backs of the four departing riders. 'Good thing we brought along plenty of bait.'

'I just hope the rain holds off,' Mo said. 'Them clouds are looking about as black as the inside of a gun barrel.'

'Let's move,' Tracker ordered. 'We need to get in position in case the shooting starts. Once we pinpoint that jasper, we'll cut him down like a three-legged deer.'

*

Latimer was nestled among the rocks below a sizeable cliff, stationed some fifty feet above the sprawling dell floor with a clear line of fire. He had never shot anyone from ambush. While riding as a stage guard he had always been in the position of defending himself or the coach. He put the notion to the back of his mind. These men had come to kill him. The only way to get justice in Baxterville was to eliminate or arrest every one of the men responsible.

There was a thick haze floating through the hills, a preamble for the heavy clouds that were moving in. The scent of rain permeated the air and the wind picked up. There was no doubt: a major storm was about to engulf the mountain range. He prayed the rain would hold off long enough for him to cut down the number of men on his trail.

Movement from the tree line below caught his eye. He put the rifle to his shoulder and took aim. However, only four riders appeared, moving along the route he had taken. Latimer reared back at the sight and looked swiftly around. He would have expected that one or more of the men following would be experienced enough to decipher his plan. The others could be anywhere – possibly closing in on his position at this very moment.

Faced with either trying to slip away without being seen and continuing to run, or making an attempt to reduce the odds against him, he decided upon the latter. Even if the rest of the posse planned to trap him, they would have to guess where he was stationed. They had to wait until he opened fire to know where he was, then move to a position where they could shoot at him. The argument sounded good in his head, but he had no idea of the caliber of the hunters after him. They might be sitting high on the mountain slope with buffalo rifles, patiently waiting for the first puff of smoke from his rifle.

Latimer took one more quick scan of the nearby hills. He had made his decision; this was his one chance to cut the odds against him. If he didn't take advantage of the opportunity, he might not get another.

The four riders were spread out, moving at a rapid pace, ready to break for cover if fired upon. Latimer picked the one closest to the best ground cover, a patch of rocks and tall brush. He hoped that by choosing him he might have a chance at getting a second man before the remaining three were able to get to safety.

Aligning his sights, he allowed for the wind, slope and distance, regarding his foe like he would have a deer or elk. Holding his breath, he squeezed the trigger gently.

Like most men who are proficient with a gun, he knew when he had made a good shot. Latimer immediately sought a second target. As the first man spilled from his saddle, the others ducked over their horses' necks and bolted for the nearest shelter.

Latimer fired twice more and was fairly certain he hit another of the remaining riders.

Before he could ascertain the second man's condition, a hail of lead rained down from above, peppering the surrounding rocks and whistling past his head. The trackers had predicted where he would be. Latimer was trapped in the rocks with hot lead flying around him like a swarm of angry wasps.

CHAPTER ELEVEN

Latimer scrambled backwards and ducked below the surface of the outcropping boulders. Bullets screamed off of the stone surfaces, sending chips of rock and dust flying. The missing gang members had got above him and that wasn't good. He risked a single hasty peek up the mountainside and spied smoke from the attackers' rifles. The look cost him a nick to one cheek from a flying rock chip. He sank down at once and rubbed at the sting. It hadn't broken the skin and, thankfully, had missed his eye, though by less than an inch. Time was not on his side. Unless he got away quickly, the men above would move until they were in position to hit him. He had to escape or die.

Seeking a safe path, Latimer went down to his belly and began to slither like a snake, remaining as low as he could get. He pushed and writhed his way back through the taller mass of the rock formation.

Reaching a tangle of scrub brush, he started to crawl for the hollow where he had left his horse. Before he managed the hundred or so feet, one of the riflemen spotted his mount. A shot echoed through the hills and the magnificent mare reared up in surprise. She bucked and squealed in pain, before losing control of her legs and falling to the ground. The fatally wounded mare thrashed about for a few seconds and then lay still.

Latimer cursed his feeble plan of attack. He had stopped two of the gang, but now was on foot and could see no ready escape. He hugged the rocky shelf, kept a low profile and scooted along until he reached a lofty crag that offered a jutting overhang for protection. Confident he could not be seen from above, he circled about and approached the dead horse from an angle of concealment. Risking a bullet between the shoulders, Latimer quickly darted forth and grabbed the canteen and saddlebags. Then, with his rifle in one hand and the bags over his shoulder, he carefully made his way to the leeward side of the slope.

The shooters from higher up were busy maneuvering for a better shot. Latimer heard someone call from below, then a voice answered from well up the mountainside. The two groups hollered back and forth, trying to determine exactly where Latimer was at.

Surveying the area and his situation, Latimer reasoned that the most logical route was to stay about halfway up the slope and move to the east. There was a huge gorge in that direction. A cautious man might be able to wind a path through the brush and trees and hide from his pursuers in the depths of the ravine. To remain where he was, within a confined area, trapped by hills on either side and a sheer cliff at his back, was nothing short of suicidal.

Latimer was still weighing his chances when Nature decided to lend a hand. The massive clouds closed in quickly. Ranging from dark gray to an angry color of black soot, the ominous tempest laid siege to the mountainous region like a mighty roiling ball of liquid fire, drenching rain and exploding thunderclaps. This was the kind of storm cattlemen hated, a true stampede starter. Such lightning and thunderstorms were fearsome and deadly in this part of Wyoming and the Dakotas. For Latimer, this particular storm might just be a life saver.

As the first drops of rain began to splatter against the dusty soil Marco risked crossing the open ground to check on his friend. Cowlick hadn't moved since going down. He turned the man's body enough to see that the first shot fired had been extremely accurate.

'Right through the heart,' Marco growled. 'Damn that Latimer!'

'Rivers caught a slug too.' Santeen spoke up from a short way off. 'The bullet hit him just below the shoulder blade. He needs a doctor pronto.'

Marco looked toward the cliff at the head of the canyon. 'The Doolan boys threw a lot of lead at Latimer. The man might be dead or wounded. If not, he is on the run.' He swore bitterly. 'Blast the man's deadly aim! Latimer only managed three shots from way up there in the rocks and he managed to hit two of us.'

'Rivers is losing a lot of blood from his wound. We've got to get him to town.'

Marco moved over and hunkered down next to Rivers. The man gritted his teeth against the pain. Santeen had wrapped a bandanna around the wounded shoulder, but it was already soaked with blood.

'Can you make it back to town on your own?' Marco asked Rivers.

'I don't know,' he admitted candidly. 'I'm already feeling light-headed. I might pass out before I get out of these hills.'

'I'm going to take him,' Santeen stated firmly. 'The Doolans will run Latimer to ground. I heard them yell down that they had killed his horse.'

'Speaking of horses, did you happen to see where Cowlick's mount went?'

'Likely spooked when he was knocked off its back,' Santeen surmised. 'I reckon he is on his way back to town by this time.'

Marco stood up straight as a rider came across the

open ground in a lope. It was Jugs Doolan. He pulled up a few feet away and looked down at the bleeding man. A distant flash of light caused him to cast a nervous glance skyward.

'Got two of you?' he asked, unlashing his poncho from behind his saddle.

'Cowlick never knew what hit him,' Marco replied. 'Rivers is going to need help to get back to the doctor.'

'Tracker and Mo are closing in on Latimer. He's afoot and running for his life.' Jugs pulled on the poncho and predicted, 'If the storm doesn't get too bad, we'll bag him.'

'Nothing is going to stop us from getting soaked,' Marco remarked, tipping his head in the direction of the black clouds. 'The rain is really going to bust loose in a minute. Won't anyone be able to track Latimer once the downpour starts.'

'I'm supposed to join up with you and cut off Latimer's escape,' Jugs reported. 'We figure he'll make for that big ravine east of the cliff.'

Marco stared up at the escarpment from where Latimer had fired on them. The rocky ledge was halfway up a near-solid wall of rock, rising up a hundred feet or more. It would have been suicide for a man to try and climb up or down that face. Even if he didn't fall to his death, he would have been exposed to gunfire from those above and below. There was only route open to Latimer.

'All right,' Marco said. 'I will join you, Jugs, and we'll get ahead of our rabbit.' He looked at the other two men. 'Without his horse, we can't very well take Cowlick back to town for burial. Santeen, throw a little dirt over his body and then take Rivers back to town.'

Even as he gave the order the wind and rain increased. A short way off in the distance the storm loomed like a vaguely translucent metallic wall, rapidly closing in on them. In five minutes or less the entire valley and mountain range would be engulfed in torrential rain, deadly lightning strikes and gales of wind.

Konrad's eyes burned from lack of sleep and his shoulders bowed beneath the weight of his weary bones. His party spied Baxterville late in the afternoon, as rain began to sprinkle. The shower grew stronger and pelted the earth with large drops of water, quickly turning the dust to mud. Soon the gusts of wind combined with a major downpour of water that spilled like a waterfall from the heavens. Konrad and his three men urged the last speed from their mounts and took cover in Brinkerhoff's barn.

'Sis is going to scald our hides,' Sheldon complained to Konrad, once they had stripped the gear from their horses. 'We're sitting out the storm while Latimer is running for his life.'

'Latimer and the gang chasing him will all be

holed up with this weather,' Konrad replied. 'Plus, we have no idea where there are.'

Brinkerhoff entered the barn with a pot of coffee and several tin cups. 'This is a good barn with a sound roof and there's plenty of straw around,' he said. 'You can hang up your wet duds to dry and get a little rest until the rain lets up.'

'Any word on Latimer?' Sheldon asked.

'Not since Milburn sent his band of killers after him.'

'You said in the telegram that there were several men on his trail?' Konrad asked, to confirm.

'The Doolan boys – two brothers and their cousin – along with Milburn's four goons, seven altogether. The Doolans are a bad trio and have done their share of man-hunting. Latimer is going to have his work cut out just to stay alive.'

'Along with Dewitt, I brought Pusher and Kates from Rimrock, but I might need more men.'

'Sam and me will ride with you as soon as he arrives with the stage tomorrow. That would make five, plus you.'

'Thanks, Brinkerhoff. I was counting on you and Sam both.'

'Yes, but where do we start?' Sheldon wanted to know. 'If Latimer is on the run, how will we find him?'

Konrad shrugged. 'From the looks of the weather, we won't be going anywhere until tomorrow morning. As for me, I've got to get some sleep or I won't be any help to Latimer or to anyone else.'

Brinkerhoff said, 'I'll have the wife make a pot of chilli. Hopefully, with this rain, Milburn didn't see you ride in. It wouldn't do for him to send someone to warn his gang that help has arrived for Latimer.'

'I didn't see anyone on the streets,' Konrad said. 'Regardless, we'll have a bite to eat, then try to dry out and get some sleep. There's nothing we can do until tomorrow.'

Visibility dropped to a few feet. Lightning struck with blazing flashes of light, followed at once with booming cracks of thunder. The ground positively shook under Nature's explosive barrage. The heavens opened up and released a deluge of water, while the wind blew cold and harsh throughout the hills.

Latimer took refuge under an overhang, semi-sheltered by the concavity of the rocky mountain wall, and waited out the worst of the storm's fury. He was about 300 yards from the nearest ridge of the ravine, but he had decided against trying to escape in that direction. He knew he was up against experienced trackers: they would undoubtedly be prepared for that. He had to do the unexpected.

The sheets of rain continued and puddles turned to streams. Within minutes the water was rushing down the numerous washes and draws. Latimer figured the lower run-off ditches would collect the various streams and become miniature floods. Having seen these storms before, he knew that once the sky cleared, the arid land would soak up the moisture and, within a matter of hours, there would only be a lingering dampness as proof that there had been any rain at all. Such was the soil in these Wyoming mountains.

Latimer remained huddled for a short time, then, weathering the steady downpour, he risked moving to the rim of the precipice. Peering down through the veil of water, he spotted two men and their horses on the valley floor. One was tossing a few rocks on something down in a cavity near a run-off ditch. It occurred to him that it was a quick burial. The reason not to take the dead man back was easy to understand – his horse had disappeared.

Some distance away, nearing the lower end of the west side of the ravine were two more riders. They were moving slowly, but would soon make their way up the ravine and pin Latimer between the two hunting parties. He now had only four men to deal with, but these were seasoned hunters and good shots. Even being an excellent marksman, he couldn't hope to get all of them before they got him.

Latimer started to back away from the lip of the rim when he noticed the movement of a dark shadow. It was in a small cove, some distance from where the impromptu burial was taking place.

Squinting hard against the blurred image, he made it out to be the missing horse. It had run off during the shooting and had found both shelter and some grass to eat. Hidden from view of anyone on the valley floor, the animal would probably wait out the storm where he was.

Latimer began to turn over ideas in his mind. If the storm lasted until nightfall, if he could manage to stay hidden until then, and if he could evade detection, he might manage an escape. A lot of ifs, and it meant working and risking his life throughout the night, but it was his best and perhaps only chance to survive.

It was not yet daylight when Brinkerhoff entered the barn and gently prodded Konrad awake. Shaking the sleep and stiffness from his body, Konrad sat up as Brinkerhoff hunkered down to speak to him.

'There was no need to wake you during the night,' Brinkerhoff explained, 'but two of the men from the posse arrived shortly after dark. Cowlick has been killed and Rivers is wounded. He's in pretty bad shape. Doc overheard Santeen telling Sheriff Milburn about the fight.'

Konrad saw concern etched in Brinkerhoff's face. 'Tell me,' he coaxed the man.

'Latimer ambushed the posse to cut the odds, but the Doolan boys were on the alert. As soon as Latimer opened up they were able to fire back at

him. Sounds as if they were ready for him and pep-
pered his hiding-place with a lot of lead. Santeen
didn't know if they had hit him or not, but they did
kill his horse and now have him trapped up on the
ledge of a sizeable cliff. They were going to surround
his position, wait out the storm, then move in for the
kill this morning.'

'How far away is it to this place?'

'It's about twenty miles, a place known as Alkali
Basin off to the north-west. It's rugged country and
there is a pretty fair bluff at the head of the valley.
I've been up that way hunting a time or two.' He
sighed. 'It's at least a six hour ride, and that's in good
weather and with dry ground.'

'Did it rain all night?'

'Pretty much. The clouds are mostly gone this
morning, but it'll take hours for the trail to dry out.'

Konrad thought aloud. 'So one man is dead, one
wounded and another brought him back to town.
Latimer cut the odds to four to one.'

'Yeah,' Brinkerhoff said, 'but three of those are
the Doolan boys. They are professional man-hunters.
Latimer is going to have his hands full trying to
match firepower against them.'

Konrad made his decision. 'Me and Pusher and
Kates will be ready to ride at daylight. Sheldon can
wait here for his sister and be on hand if Latimer
should make it back on his own.'

'I'll bring something over for breakfast,'

Brinkerhoff said. 'Then the wife and Mr Dewitt can watch over the express office until we return. You need someone to show you the way.'

The other three men had awoken at the first sound of voices. They had been listening to the conversation and now gathered around to voice their agreement with the plan. As soon as Brinkerhoff left, Sheldon gave Konrad a serious look.

'You're not having me stay behind because I'm a tenderfoot?'

Konrad chuckled. 'No, Mr Dewitt. It's because you are the only one here who has any chance of stopping your sister from getting a gun and trying to follow after us.' He added: 'Besides which, with your father being a banker, you're much better equipped to help with the office duties than any of us.'

'Marshal's right,' Pusher spoke up. 'Kates and me can't read.'

Sheldon displayed a grim humor. 'You put forth a good argument, but I'm betting the truth is, the three of you are scared to death of having to face Constance when she arrives.'

'Guilty as charged,' Pusher admitted. 'You sister's all yours!'

Tracker was up and watching long before daylight. Eventually he could make out a few dark outlines of the rough terrain. The air was cool, but the clouds were mostly gone. The sun would shine today and make short work of drying out the land.

Mo came over to stand at the lookout point that Tracker had chosen. It was a rocky perch that offered a view of both the valley below and the entire rock face of the nearby cliff.

'You still think he's somewhere among the rocks?' Mo asked.

'Hard tuh say,' Tracker replied. 'We threw a lot of lead at him. It's possible we nicked him a time or two. Might be he's wounded so he can't go very far.'

'Yeah, but he wouldn't just sit there, big brother. The man has to know we would send a couple men up the ravine and trap him between us.'

Tracker, who always thought before he spoke, took a bite from a plug of tobacco. After crushing it with his teeth, he shifted it to the left side of his mouth between his cheek and gum. After some moments he made his observation. 'We kilt his hoss, so he's afoot. The gent also considers himself to be a hell of a rifleman. As proof, he done hit two of our number with only three shots, and he done it from a coupla hundred yards with a fair amount of wind.' Tracker paused to spit a stream of juice. 'I'm betting he is fortified in a hole somewhere close and is going to try and shoot it out with us.'

Mo grunted his contempt at the idea. 'Four of us against only him? Man would have to be crazy to—'

Tracker suddenly grabbed his arm. Mo threw a quizzical glance at his brother, then followed where

Tracker was looking.

'It's him!' Tracker whispered. 'See? Out there between the rocks, at the rim of the ledge?'

Mo stared hard against the dim light of dawn. 'I see him!' Mo replied excitedly. 'He's checking the valley floor, trying to figure what direction we'll hit him from.'

'Stupid stunt, exposing himself that-a-way.'

Mo retrieved his rifle while Tracker readied his own weapon. As Mo returned, he said quietly, 'Bet he thinks the darkness is enough to hide his taking a gander at his situation.'

'That will be the last mistake he makes, little brother,' Tracker vowed. 'We fire together. Don't give him no chance to duck back down in those rocks.'

Both men were excellent shots and they had worked together all their lives. When Tracker started the countdown, Mo adjusted the rhythm of his breathing to match that of his brother.

'Three . . . two . . . one!'

Both men pulled their triggers at the same instant, each of them confident his aim was true.

Two slugs slammed into the body of the man surveying the valley below. The force of two bullets striking his body knocked him forward and over the ledge. There was a short wail, a death cry that ended abruptly when the man hit the bottom of the precipice.

CHAPTER TWELVE

'Hot damn!' Mo shouted. 'We sure enough put an end to that troublesome jasper.'

'Let's have us a look,' Tracker said. 'Maybe we can see where he landed.'

The two of them gathered up their horses and headed down the side of the mountain. When they reached a clearing that allowed them to see the base of the cliff, they knew any further search was a waste of time.

'Landed in the run-off going down that wash,' Tracker remarked. 'His body will likely be carried for miles.'

'Bet the water's running six feet deep where he fell,' Mo agreed. 'We'll never find him.'

A single shot came from a quarter-mile away, up along the ridge of the ravine. It was Jugs, signaling to find out what had happened. Mo pulled his handgun and fired three evenly spaced shots to give him the all clear.'

Tracker speculated, 'Reckon we'll meet Marco and Jugs at the mouth of the canyon. We'll have to navigate around the different run-off streams, but I figure we'll all get there at about the same time.'

'I'm ready,' Mo said. 'It's been one cold, wet, miserable night. I could do with a hot meal and a warm, dry bed.'

'You're becoming sissified,' Tracker teased.

Mo grinned. 'I seen you shivering a few times last night, too.'

'Let's get off of this blasted hill and make some time. It's gonna be noon or later before we reach town.'

The ground was drying out quickly from mud to being mostly damp by the time Konrad saw the group of riders coming their way. He held up his hand to stop his men and waited for the four horsemen to draw closer. Brinkerhoff identified the men for Konrad before the group came to a stop.

'I'm a United States marshal,' he introduced himself to the foursome. 'I'm looking for Dean Latimer.'

Tracker paused to spit a stream of tobacco juice before replying. 'Yer too late, Marshal,' he said smugly. 'Latimer ambushed us yesterday, but he was a mite careless this morning. Mo and me knocked him off a cliff, with a bullet each. He fell about a hundred feet into one of the gullies. Weren't no chance to recover his body. He'll likely float down that dirty river of water and wash up out on the prairie flatlands somewhere.'

'You killed him?' Brinkerhoff asked the unnecessary question.

'He kilt one of our own and shot another yesterday,' Tracker retorted. 'The man was wanted for murder in Baxterville. He done kilt the banker.'

Konrad put a hard look on Marco. 'We only have your word that Latimer did the killing,' he challenged.

'Seen the whole thing, Marshal,' Marco said innocently. 'Ain't no doubt he shot poor old Bellows.'

'Same as the banker seeing young Dewitt kill the rancher,' Konrad commented. 'Curious the way you fellows have a habit of always having an eyewitness when someone is killed up in this part of the country.'

Marco's eyes danced with disdain, but he kept it out of his voice. 'Tell you the truth, Marshal, I was keeping an eye on the banker. Sheriff Milburn wasn't sure why he had lied to everyone, but it seemed a possibility that he was trying to steal Mr Graham's horse ranch.'

'That's why you were outside his house?'

'Yep,' Marco reported. 'When I heard two men arguing I moved over to get a better look. Before I could do anything to stop him Latimer gunned

Bellows down.'

'According to the doc, Bellows was shot in the back.' Brinkerhoff sounded off.

Marco didn't flinch. 'Yeah, the frightened devil tried to run from the room but Latimer was too quick. I shot through the glass window trying to hit Latimer, but he got out the back way and escaped.'

Konrad glowered at the man. 'You tell a good story, Marco, but it sounds more like a fairy tale to me.'

Marco only grinned, while Tracker spat a stream of juice and started forward. 'You got more questions, Marshal, you can ask them in town. Me and the boys spent a cold, wet night out in the hills. We're heading for a good meal and some shut-eye.'

Konrad didn't reply, but neither did he try to stop the four of them from riding past. He stared off into the distance unseeing until Brinkerhoff nudged his leg with the toe of his boot.

'If they told us straight, we'll likely never find Latimer's body. I've been out this way after a hard rain. The washes and gullies run fast and deep for hours afterwards.'

'Fell from a cliff, too,' Pusher interjected. 'I can't see any way a man could survive being shot, knocked off a cliff, and then swept away in a raging river.'

Konrad groaned. 'I'd rather take a beating than have to tell Miss Dewitt that we were too late to help. She's gonna scald my hide.'

'Nothing we could have done,' Brinkerhoff said. 'Latimer took a big chance by coming back. His trying to get to the truth of Graham's death cost him his life.'

'I don't suppose we could find Latimer's body unless we spent a week looking,' Konrad admitted sadly. 'Let's head back to town.'

Because of the muddy road conditions the stage didn't arrive until sundown. Sam hadn't even brought the team to a full stop when the door of the coach flew open. Constance did an unladylike jump to the ground before Sheldon could get there to help her down.

Konrad remained back a short way, figuring her brother owed Latimer a bigger debt than he did himself. If Sheldon took the brunt of the lady's fury, he could then console her by telling her how sorry he was and that he would continue to look into the death of the banker and Graham.

However, their fears of hysteria or ire were unfounded. Instead of exploding in a temperamental rage, Constance took one look at Sheldon's sorrowful expression and ran to him. He held her as she cried against his shoulder.

'We got here too late to help,' Sheldon lamented quietly. 'Latimer got two of the men following him, but the odds against him were too great.'

'He . . .' she murmured between sobs, 'he was the

first man I ever met who . . .' But she could not keep her throat from constricting.

'I know,' Sheldon said gently, rubbing her back lightly with one hand. 'I know, Sis.'

Deciding it was safe to approach, Konrad removed his hat and moved to within a few feet. 'Latimer was the kind of man this country needs,' he proclaimed candidly. 'He felt a duty to take on a job I hadn't even assigned him. I asked him to come here and try to save an innocent man's life. I didn't expect him to try to solve a murder case too.'

Constance gathered her composure and stepped away from her brother. With more aplomb than Konrad expected, she faced him with a controlled demeanor. 'I don't blame you, Marshal. I know Dean did this on his own. He was . . .' she gulped to suppress a sob, before finishing. 'He was that kind of man.'

'He was a very good man,' Konrad concurred. 'I'm sorry it turned out this way.'

'I got you the same room at the hotel,' Sheldon told her, deciding they had said all they could about Latimer. 'If you would like to get something to eat first, I can—'

'No.' She declined before he finished. 'I don't feel much like eating. I think I'd prefer to be alone for a while.'

'Go ahead, Sis. I'll get your Saratoga and bring it to your room.'

Staring through a veil of tears, Constance walked numbly down the street to the hotel. Latimer had been a shining knight, a genuine hero and protector. She had envisioned a great many fantasies with Dean, even a life together. He would have been a strong, able, loving man, one she could admire and be proud of. How could she continue, knowing the first man she had ever wanted in her life was gone?

Milburn was satisfied by the Doolan boys and Marco's report. It was a relief to have Latimer out of the way, but there were other concerns. Bellows had been up to something before he died. Marco had overheard the man confessing what he knew of Graham's murder and had done what was necessary, but there was more to this.

Janus came by for a visit and update, so Milburn filled him in about the battle out at Alkali Basin. He also brought him up to date on Marshal Ellington and his men.

'They've got no reason to stick around,' Janus said testily. 'Unless the marshal wants to open an investigation about Amble Graham's death.' He paused to grin at Milburn. 'With Francis being the only witness and him being dead, we all know he will never find anything out on that subject.'

'I'm more concerned with what our banker partner was doing,' Milburn replied. 'Latimer managed to escape on Francis's prize Arabian horse.

Yet, when I spoke to Brinkerhoff, he told me it was Francis himself who had picked up his horse that morning.'

'That morning?' Janus was no longer smug. 'Why would he have done that? Do you think he knew Latimer was coming back?'

'How could he? Hap and the boys were watching both him and Latimer. Neither of them was out of our sight until Latimer boarded the stage. He obviously got off the coach down the trail a piece and doubled back.'

Janus snorted. 'Blast that interfering Latimer! He about ruined everything.'

'Yes, but what was Francis up to? How come he had his horse hidden out back of his house, and where was he going? He told Bill Riley he was leaving town, but he never said if or when he was coming back.'

Janus suddenly paled. 'What about the deed to Graham's ranch?'

Milburn shrugged. 'I didn't ask.' At the stormy glare from Janus, he bridled. 'Look, I can't go asking about the banker's dealings, not when we had Graham killed to get our hands on his property.'

'Well, I can!' Janus exploded. 'I'm the judge of this here town. It's my duty to see that no one swindles that deed from our grasp.'

'The deed belonged to the bank,' Milburn reminded him. 'We have no claim to the horse ranch. Our deal was with Francis.'

'But . . .' Janus was shaking with rage. 'But it's ours! We planned everything so we could gain control of that land.'

'And Francis died before he could sign anything over to the corporation we were going to form.'

'That stupid Marco!' Janus fumed. 'He went and killed the only man who could have kept our agreement.'

Milburn waved a hand to make the man simmer down. 'Take a deep breath, Judge,' he told him. 'Changing your complexion from ash-coloured to crimson so quick will sure enough bring on apoplexy. We can still pick up the deed. Soon as the marshal and the Dewitts are out of our hair, we'll form the corporation and invite Riley to join. If he doesn't, we can approach Lou Pine. His saloon does a good business. I'm sure he'd fork over the money to get in on something like this.'

'All right, Sheriff,' Janus said, the redness of his face beginning to fade. 'Once things are back to normal we'll go have a nice talk with Riley. Being suddenly in charge of the bank, I imagine, even if he chooses not to join our little association, he will be happy to sell the ranch at a reasonable price.'

'Right you are, Janus. I'll talk to you later.'

The judge left the office and Hap passed him at the door. 'Rivers died a few minutes ago,' he announced. 'Doc said he had lost too much blood,

142

and being soaked to the bone by that storm didn't help none.'

Milburn bobbed his head in acknowledgement, but he groaned inside. Latimer had been one large thorn in his side. He arrived to save Sheldon Dewitt and then spooked Francis into doing something stupid. Next he manages to elude escape until he's killed two of his hired men and also involved the US marshal. The man was the embodiment of cholera, striking people down with a mixture of fear and death.

Damn the man's interference! Everything was going great until he showed up.

Constance was roused from her sleep by a soft tapping at her door. She groaned and blinked to soothe her burning eyes. Greeted by the gloomy interior of the room, she realized she had cried herself to sleep and it was after dark. How late it was she didn't know.

'Just a minute,' she said hoarsely. Lethargically shaking the cobwebs from her brain she got off of the bed and fumbled to find the room's lamp. There were matches next to it so she struck one and lit the wick. As the room became bathed in light, she adjusted the lamp and moved over to the door. She opened it, expecting to see Shelly, probably worried that she hadn't left her room to eat. He was naturally concerned that she might. . . .

Constance gawked, her heart stopped, and she was stunned to speechlessness. Standing in the hallway was Dean Latimer.

CHAPTER THIRTEEN

'What. . . ?' The lady stumbled away from Latimer in shock. He quickly entered her room and closed the door.

Constance shook her head in disbelief. 'They told me you were dead.'

Latimer knew his appearance did little to alter the validity of that statement. He was dirty, unshaven and haggard from not sleeping for the past forty-eight hours. The hat on his head didn't quite fit and the shirt and jacket he wore had belonged to Cowlick.

'I'm sorry about—' he began.

'Have you been shot?' Constance cried, alarmed by the dried blood on his shirtfront.

'No, I borrowed these clothes.'

Without another word Constance flew into his arms and hugged him tightly. After a few seconds she pushed back and surveyed Latimer from head to foot.

'You're not hurt at all? No broken bones? No bloody stumps?'

Latimer displayed a tight grin. 'I managed to escape with all of my body parts intact.'

A sudden, unexpected slap from Constance's right palm stung his cheek, instantly removing his smirk. The swat was hard enough to bring tears to his eyes and caused him to take an involuntary step backward.

'How dare you do that to me!' She tore into him with a harsh, scathing voice. 'Do you have any idea of how I felt?' She lifted her hand as if she would swing at him a second time.

Latimer dodged away, throwing up both hands to ward off a second attack. 'Whoa there, miss!' He tried to calm her, 'I didn't mean to—'

'I never want to feel that way again.' She silenced his excuse. 'Do you hear me? Never!'

'I'm sorry,' he said, talking quickly. 'I was trapped. I had to fake my death to keep from getting killed.'

Rather than continue to assault him physically, Constance slipped past his guard, wrapped her arms about him and hugged him tightly a second time. After a long moment, she leaned back and kissed him. Paralysed by the delightful contact, Latimer tried to get his emotions on to a level plane. After a few blissful seconds the woman removed herself from the embrace, walked over and sat down on the bed.

'All right,' she said, by now a portrait of composure, 'tell me what happened.'

Latimer explained about attempting to lessen the odds and ending up being trapped on the rocky ledge. With a dead horse and no way of escape, he knew they would get him once the storm cleared.

'So I used the hard rain and blackness of night for cover. I could have tried to escape and come back to town, but I couldn't be sure they weren't watching the trail. I might have ridden into an ambush. I decided the only safe bet was to let them think they had killed me.

'It took me all night but I managed to find Cowlick's horse and recover his body. By moving slow and careful, I got back up to the ledge well before daylight.' He shrugged, as if the rest of the story would explain itself. When Constance narrowed her neatly trimmed eyebrows in a silent command, he finished the tale.

'I changed clothes with Cowlick and dragged him to the rim of the ledge. I posed him in the rocks and fixed a couple of sticks on a length of rawhide to prop up his body. When the Doolan boys opened fire, I yanked the sticks out from under Cowlick's body and he pitched over the cliff.' He shrugged. 'I even gave a little holler, as if I had gone over the side.'

Constance frowned. Latimer stood there, feeling like a schoolboy who had been summoned to stay in

147

school after class. He swallowed his anxiety and patiently waited for her to say something. She studied him for a time, as if wondering what kind of man would think up such a stunt. After a few moments of silence, she cleared her throat.

'So now what?' she asked.

'I need to get a few hours' sleep. Then Konrad and me will arrest everyone involved in the murder of Amble Graham and Francis Bellows.'

'Just like that?'

Latimer tipped his head to the side in a nonchalant fashion. 'Pretty much.'

Somewhat timorously, she queried, 'What about the two of us?'

Latimer smiled. 'I'll be around to talk to you about that . . . but not while I'm dog tired, covered in dirt and grime and still have a half-dozen men to bring to justice.'

'If you get yourself killed . . . for real this time,' she added pointedly, 'I won't cry or mourn your death. I did that already. I shan't be as weepy and maudlin a second time.'

'I'm the proudest man on earth to think you would shed a tear on my behalf,' Latimer replied seriously. 'There's no way a few gunmen are going to stop me from coming back for you.'

Constance allowed a winsome smile to play along her lips. 'I'll hold you to that, Dean Latimer.'

*

Konrad and Sheldon were at the spare room at the express office when Latimer awoke the next morning. Brinkerhoff arrived with a bowl of oatmeal and a cup of coffee before Latimer had rubbed the sleep from his eyes.

'You really think this is the play to make?' Konrad asked.

Latimer had spoken to him about his idea the previous night, before he fell into a deep, exhausted slumber. He sipped at the coffee and then began to eat the nicely warmed oatmeal.

'I think it'll work,' he replied between mouthfuls. He looked at Brinkerhoff for support.

'Santeen, Rivers, Cowlick and Marco were all playing cards when Graham was killed,' the man reported. 'The judge and Milburn were also in the saloon at the time.' He snorted, 'Convenient alibis if not for being so obvious.'

'Which means the Doolan boys likely killed Graham,' Latimer postulated. 'We need proof . . . or someone who will testify against them all in court.'

'You finish eating and get cleaned up,' Konrad told Latimer. 'Sam brought you a change of clothes and a shaving kit. Soon as you're ready, take the creek trail and meet us at the banker's house. No one will expect us to meet there and it's far enough from town, so we shouldn't be seen.'

Brinkerhoff asked, 'You want Sam and me to come along?'

Konrad shook his head. 'Better keep watch on the opposition until we find out if this is going to work. I'll get in touch when we are ready to make our move.'

As the marshal and the others filed out of the barn, Latimer finished off the bowl of oatmeal and downed the last of the coffee. A quick washing, a shave and a change of clothes and he began to look and feel like his old self. He took time to oil his gun and put in fresh loads. He hoped there wouldn't be any shooting, but it paid to be prepared.

Hap entered the sheriff's office with a puzzled look on his face. Milburn had been discussing business with Marco and Tracker. Those two men ceased talking when the deputy entered.

'We're kind of busy here, Hap,' Milburn told his less than keen deputy.

'Something funny happened, Sheriff,' Hap replied. 'I thought you ought to know about it.'

Milburn was impatient. 'As I said, we're quite busy.'

Hap looked cowed, as if he were being scolded, but remained standing with his head lowered – an obedient dog, uncertain as to whether to approach or retreat.

'All right, Hap.' Milburn relented. 'What is it?'

'The marshal just took Santeen out of the saloon. It looked like he was arresting him or something.'

'What?' Milburn cried. Hap had his complete attention now. 'Tell me about it.'

'Well, Konrad and those two men who come with him to town, they showed up at the saloon.' He took a breath. 'I was having lunch there – you know Mr Pine has that Mexican gal fix tacos and the like three days a week.'

'Yes, yes,' Milburn said, agonizing over Hap's delay in getting to the meat of his report.

'So, anyway, I was sitting across the room. Santeen drank until he passed out last night and it looked like he was keeping the barkeep as busy as a beaver building a new dam today. I reckon he was gonna be booze-blind by dusk.'

Milburn nearly exploded with his impatience. 'All right, so he was trying to drink the Palace dry. So what about the marshal?'

'Konrad stepped right up to him and took his gun. Then he and his two deputies hauled him out of the room.'

'Where did they take him?'

'No idea, Sheriff. I come to let you know what I'd seen.'

Milburn exchanged looks with Marco and Tracker. 'All right, Hap,' he said, withholding the concern from his voice. 'Keep an eye on things and let me know if anything else happens.'

'You got it, Sheriff,' Hap said eagerly. 'I'll sure keep an eye peeled.'

As soon as the door had closed Tracker said, 'I don't like it. Santeen is liable to spill his guts and we'll all be looking down the marshal's gun barrel.'

'Santeen won't talk,' Milburn assured him.

But Marco wasn't so sure. 'He was already draining bottles this morning, and he was so liquored up last night he couldn't find the floor with both hands. Him and Rivers were like brothers. Betwixt the snake poison and grief, his mouth might start talking before his brain can siphon through all the whiskey he's drunk.'

Milburn frowned in thought. 'We can't kill a United States marshal.'

'The hell we can't!' Tracker sneered. 'If that badge comes looking for us Doolans, he'll be putting nails in his own coffin.'

'I think we ought to put a man or two in place to watch our backs . . . just in case,' Marco suggested.

'All right.' Milburn gave in. 'You take care of it and the rest of us will meet right here. If it comes to a fight, we'll have the advantage in strategy and numbers.'

Shortly before noon Konrad and his two deputies approached the jail. Milburn had evidently been watching as he and Tracker and Mo Doolan came out on the porch to meet them. While they showed no open hostility, all three men had their gunhands on the butts of their revolvers.

152

'I'm told you arrested one of my hired men.' Milburn opened the conversation. 'Mind telling me why?'

'Actually, I didn't arrest Santeen,' Konrad replied. 'He was very cooperative and isn't being charged with any crimes. He seemed to talk a lot more freely when he learned that you didn't have the deed to Graham's horse ranch after all.' Konrad let the news sink in, then added: 'Can't say it will go as easy on Janus Poe. He's under arrest for murder.'

'You arrested the judge?' Milburn was more surprised than upset. 'How does he figure into a murder?'

'Same as you and the Doolans,' Konrad said casually. 'You killed Amble Graham for his ranch. Then Marco killed Francis Bellows when he thought he was about to talk to Latimer.' He hardened his stance. 'By the way, Latimer was acting as my deputy at the time.'

'Latimer didn't say anything to me about being a deputy marshal, and you can't prove a thing.' Milburn was arrogant. 'After all, Francis was the only witness to Graham's death and only Marco and Latimer were with Francis at the time of his death.'

Another man came into view, walking across from the saddle and hardware store. Milburn could not stop his mouth from falling open. It was Latimer!

'Marco was fixing to waylay us from atop the store,' Latimer announced to Konrad. 'I left him trussed up

153

like a Thanksgiving turkey.' With a cocky grin he added: 'These look like the only three turkeys left.'

'It ain't possible that you're alive!' Tracker wailed. 'My brother and I both put slugs in you. We seen you tumble over the cliff!'

Latimer sighed. 'Sorry to disappoint you fellows, but Cowlick took that fall for me. He was thoughtful enough to provide me with a horse, too. I'm right grateful for his help, because we wanted to catch all of the murderers – you Doolans in particular.'

Tracker's upper lip curled like a snarling dog's. 'Yeah? Well, this time we won't miss!'

'Don't expect help from your cousin,' Brinkerhoff's booming voice announced, as he and Sam brought Jugs out from behind the bakery.

'That accounts for everyone,' Konrad said. 'You boys best drop your irons or we'll have to dispense justice without the benefit of a judge and jury.'

'Hold it!' another voice cried out.

Latimer didn't take his eyes off Tracker and Mo. They were the most dangerous of the three men. However, he used his peripheral vision to see that the new arrival was the deputy, Hap. He had his gun out; he was confused, but ready to side his boss.

'You don't want to get involved in this,' Brinkerhoff told him. 'Milburn ordered Graham killed and Marco killed Bellows. They did it to get the deed to Graham's ranch, but it didn't work.'

'Why would you want Graham's ranch, Sheriff?'

Hap wanted to know. 'I thought you liked being sheriff.'

'Drop the gun, Deputy.' Sheldon had come out from his place of concealment. His rifle was pointed at Hap, prompting him to drop his revolver.

In an unnatural show of compassion, Sheriff Milburn looked at his deputy. 'Don't get involved here, Hap,' he said. 'I made a mistake and I've got to pay for it.'

Those words ended the vocal part of the standoff. Suddenly, everything grew deadly still; it seemed no one breathed. The sun was high overhead, not a whisper of a breeze, with seven men facing each other. Latimer had studied men all his life. He knew Tracker was the most deadly. Konrad would know that too, but he was also aware of Latimer's superior skill with a gun. He would automatically take Mo Doolan. If a fight started, Pusher and Kates would only have to deal with Sheriff Milburn.

Who can say what causes a man to act – pride, anger, bravery, even cowardice? Whatever the impulse, Tracker and Mo both made their decision at the same instant. Konrad got out a single word of warning: 'Don't!'

But the two man-hunters pulled their guns!

Milburn threw his arms in the air to surrender, while the deadly precision of the six-gun dealt a final hand to end the stand-off.

Konrad was much quicker than Latimer might

have guessed, but his gun still went off a millisecond after Latimer's Remington. Each of them fired twice, making certain their targets had no chance to return fire.

As Tracker and Mo went down, Milburn scrambled away from their bodies, hands held high. Jugs cursed vehemently, watching his two cousins die before his eyes, but he was helpless and disarmed.

As the smoke from Konrad and Latimer's guns lingered, Hap walked up to stand next to them. He gave his head a shake, looking at the dead Doolan brothers.

'I never knew nothing about any of it, Marshal,' he said weakly. 'Guess I must be about as dumb as a kettle of rocks.'

Konrad slowly holstered his weapon and gave Hap a sidelong look. 'No, Deputy, you didn't know because you're an honest man. You trusted the sheriff to be an honest man too.'

'Do that mean I can keep being a deputy?'

'You are acting sheriff until the town can elect a new one. After that, it'll be up to the new sheriff.'

'What do I do now?' Hap asked.

Latimer was the one to answer. 'Take the prisoners inside and lock them up. I'll go get Marco and bring him over to join them.'

Brinkerhoff and the two deputies began to remove the bodies of Tracker and Mo: violent men who had died a violent death. Jugs was allowed to stop long enough to make certain both of them were dead. He sighed after the inspection.

'I knew those two would get me in trouble one day. Ma always said they was no damn good.'

Within minutes, Janus, Milburn, Marco and Jugs were behind bars. Konrad and Kates would accompany the four prisoners back to Rimrock. Santeen would take the next stage to testify. Pusher was going to stick around and help Hap until the town could appoint a new sheriff.

With everything lined out, Konrad had a private moment with Latimer. He began by pulling out a sheet of paper.

'This belongs to you,' he said. 'The banker sent it, along with his deposition about the murder of Graham.'

Latimer looked at the document. 'It looks like a deed.'

'You are now the owner of Graham's horse ranch. Francis transferred enough money to pay off the mortgage when he turned the bank over to the Rileys. I guess he thought you would get to the bottom of Graham's murder and that Graham would want you to inherit his place. Far as anyone knows the man didn't have any kin.'

'I'm not going to live on a horse ranch,' a feminine voice complained disapprovingly. 'My husband is going to be a proper gentleman.'

Latimer and the marshal turned to see that

Constance had approached without them hearing her.

'If the railroad runs a spur up north, that land will be worth a fortune,' Konrad informed Constance.

'Then we'll let my brother run the ranch until that day comes to pass.'

Konrad looked to Latimer, waiting for his response. 'Well?' he prompted, when his deputy didn't speak up.

'Seriously?' Latimer asked Konrad. 'You're expecting me to contradict a woman like Constance?'

Konrad laughed. 'Yeah, what am I thinking? You'll probably be managing a bank of your own in a year or two. That's got to beat raising a herd of mustangs and breaking them to ride.'

'I heard you talking.' Sheldon spoke up, having arrived to join the three of them. 'I think I'd do rather well running a ranch. After all, there are already two wranglers out there who do most of the gut-busting part.'

'Sounds good to me,' Latimer said. 'You get the horses and I get the girl.'

Constance furrowed her brow, but there was a playful smile on her lips. 'Not the most apposite way of asking for my hand, but I will take your lack of proper upbringing into account.'

'Fair enough,' Latimer replied. 'When it comes to upbringing, I'll let you be responsible for our children's rearing.'

Constance hooked her arm through his and laughed. 'I knew we could come to terms.'

Konrad chuckled, smiling at their entertaining exchange, and announced: 'And they both lived happily ever after.'